A NOVEL BY

TUCKER SHAW

Amulet Books · New York

Oh Yeah, Audrey!

Library of Congress Cataloging-in-Publication Data

Shaw, Tucker.
Oh Yeah, Audrey! / by Tucker Shaw.
pages cm
Summary: Months after the death of her mother, sixteen-year-old Gemma Beasley and friends she met through her Tumblr page meet in New York City to celebrate the life and style of Audrey Hepburn and her famous character, Holly Golightly.
ISBN 978-1-4197-1223-4
[1. Breakfast at Tiffany's (Motion picture)—Fiction. 2. Hepburn, Audrey, 1929–1993—Fiction. 3. New York (N.Y.)—Fiction. 4. Runaways—Fiction. 5. Friendship—Fiction. 6. Grief—Fiction.] I. Title.
PZ7.S53445Oh 2014
[Fi]c—dc23
2014001465

Text copyright © 2014 Tucker Shaw
Illustrations copyright © 2014 Malika Favre
Book design by Maria T. Middleton

Printed and bound in U.S.A.
10 9 8 7 6 5 4 3 2 1

Amulet Books are available at special discounts when purchased in quantity for premiums and promotions as well as fundraising or educational use. Special editions can also be created to specification. For details, contact specialsales@abramsbooks.com or the address below.

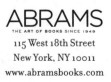

THE ART OF BOOKS SINCE 1949
115 West 18th Street
New York, NY 10011
www.abramsbooks.com

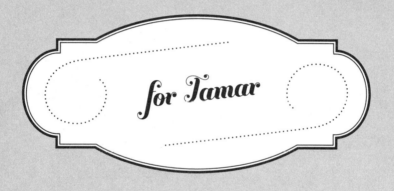

for Tamar

PROLOGUE

I t's not like I officially ran away. Actual running away is when you just can't take it anymore—your family or school or life in general—and you hop a bus to some big city, change your name, and find a job clearing plates or checking coats at a restaurant. Or worse. If you fall in with the wrong people, there's no telling what you'll end up doing. Actual running away means you don't intend to come back, ever. But that's not what I did. I always planned to go back home.

I took a train from Philadelphia to New York City last night without telling Dad. I would have told him if I'd actually seen him before I left. But he wasn't home, and I didn't have time to wait around, so I just left. He thinks I'm spending the night at my friend Casey's, which I used to do sometimes. Little does he know Casey and I haven't spoken to each other in weeks.

So, no, it wasn't running away.

That's where Audrey Hepburn and I are different. She ran away for real. She had no intention of going back to being Lulamae Barnes from Tulip, Texas. Which I can totally understand. Her life pretty much sucked back home. And so does mine.

I call her Audrey Hepburn, but really I mean Holly Golightly—you know, from *Breakfast at Tiffany's*, a.k.a. the best movie ever made. Have you seen it?

I read somewhere on the Internet that Truman Capote, the writer who created the character Holly Golightly, really wanted Marilyn Monroe to play the part. Can you imagine? Marilyn Monroe, with her platinum blond hair and little girl voice, playing Holly Golightly? No way. Audrey Hepburn, long and tall and with that way of calling everyone *dahling* . . . she's the only one who could have played that part. As far as I'm concerned, Holly Golightly and Audrey Hepburn were pretty much made for each other.

If you haven't seen *Breakfast at Tiffany's*, go to Netflix and watch it. Seriously. Right now. Or at least check out YouTube for the opening credits, which last, like, two minutes. Trust me. Besides, if you watch it, the rest of this story will make a lot more sense. Maybe you'll understand where I'm coming from. Maybe you'll understand exactly what happened. And why.

I finally did something worth writing about. The kind of thing that stories are made of. Mom would have liked that, I think. She was a writer. To her, nothing was more important than stories. Especially if they were true.

Anyway, I didn't really run away like Audrey did in the movie. Holly, I mean. But we both ended up at the same place anyway:

New York City.

Tiffany's.

For breakfast.

*J*he sun is just a vague suggestion somewhere low in the sky. A soft, pinkish light pulsing slowly across the tops of the glass-and-limestone buildings that line Fifth Avenue in Manhattan.

I can't believe I'm here.

Yes, I can.

I'm standing on the sidewalk at the corner of Fifty-seventh Street and Fifth Avenue, near the curb, just a few yards from the grand, granite-carved sign that reads: TIFFANY & CO. New York stretches into the sky above me. I'm alone here, not another soul on the street, and I swear I can hear

"Moon River" floating through the air. I close my eyes, inhale, and breathe in the city.

This is where she stood.

I'm happy for this hour alone, before the others come. If they come.

Across the sidewalk, I catch my reflection in the Tiffany's window. It's hazy, just an outline. My hair is up, just like hers, and my dress is long and sleek, just like hers. I've got the triple strand of pearls and cat's-eye sunglasses and low slingbacks with kitten heels. Opera gloves, an ivory cape slung over one arm, and a shimmering diamond tiara. If I don't look too closely, I'd swear it was Audrey Hepburn in that reflection. Tall and willowy and glamorous.

There's no trace in that hazy reflection of normal, boring, sixteen-year-old Gemma Beasley from normal, boring Philadelphia, Pennsylvania. No trace of the fake rhinestone tiara or the sixteen-dollar thrift-store gown that wouldn't even know how to pronounce *Givenchy*. It's a movie star in that window, a real one, in a real Givenchy evening gown.

I close my eyes, imprinting the image on my brain. I don't want to forget it, ever.

I'm here. I've escaped. I've transformed. I'm not Gemma. I'm Audrey. Today, I'm Audrey Hepburn.

5:05 A.M.

shiver. It's chilly, an early June morning.

I suppose I could slip on my cape.

But no, I can't put it on. I have a script to follow. *Breakfast at Tiffany's*, the opening scene, where Audrey Hepburn (a.k.a. glamorous young socialite Holly Golightly) steps out of a cab at Fifty-seventh and Fifth—Tiffany's—in the early Manhattan morning after a night out. She gazes at the jewels in the Tiffany's windows while sipping coffee from a paper cup and munching on a pastry. She looks gorgeous. "Moon River" plays in the background—that soft, melancholy song with the swelling violins—and the credits run. *Audrey Hepburn. George Peppard.*

Patricia Neal. Mickey Rooney as "Mr. Yunioshi." Based on the novel by Truman Capote. Directed by Blake Edwards.

I wonder if Audrey was cold that morning, too. I bet she was, but she never put on her cape. And so my cape stays draped over my arm even as goose bumps crawl past my elbows. Audrey didn't need hers, and neither do I.

I look around. Will anyone else come?

Stop being anxious, I say to myself. *They won't even be here until six.*

It's going to be a big day. We've been planning it for weeks and weeks.

As soon as I saw online that the Ziegfeld Theater was planning a midnight showing of *Breakfast at Tiffany's* as a way to commemorate the twentieth anniversary of Audrey Hepburn's death, I knew I had to be there.

I also knew that Dad wouldn't allow it. Hence the (so-called) running away.

Anyway, I used Google Maps to make a walking tour of landmarks from the movie and made plans (and reservations) for lunch and dinner at places Holly Golightly went to; and the marquee event—a midnight screening of *Breakfast at Tiffany's* at the Ziegfeld Theater, which is the most massive, spectacular movie theater in the entire universe—will be the cherry on the cake.

I pull a piece of paper out of my clutch.

Itinerary for the First (Annual?)

Beyond-Fabulous Breakfast at Tiffany's *Weekend!*

Saturday and Sunday, June 11–12

SATURDAY

§ 6:00 A.M. § *Meet at Tiffany's with pastries and coffee.*

§ 7:00 A.M. § *Breakfast at a Third Avenue diner.*

§ 9:00 A.M. § *Return to individual hotels to change.*

I'm staying at the Malcolm, a supercheap hotel in China-town with a shared bathroom down the hall. I'm not sure where the others are staying yet.

§ 10:00 A.M. § *Begin walking tour of* Breakfast at Tiffa-ny's *landmarks, starting at Holly's apartment building on Seventy-first Street, where she lived alone with a cat (named Cat), downstairs from the handsome Paul Varjak (who Holly insisted on calling Fred and refused to allow herself to fall in love with).* Even though both of them had dates with other people—mostly rich people who always gave them money—it was obvious they should be together.

§ 11:00 A.M. § *Continue walking tour with visit to Central Park, where Paul Varjak met up with Doc—the husband Holly left behind when she ran away from Texas. Doc still* called Holly by her old name, Lulamae Barnes, and he came to New York to convince her to come back. Holly never told Paul that she was married, of course. Not that she was trying to hide it from him or anything. I think she was just trying to forget her old life back in Texas.

§1:00 P.M.§ *Lunch at Hamburger Heaven, where Holly Golightly met Mr. O'Shaughnessy to give him the "weather report."* The weather report was coded information that Holly got from a mobster named Sally Tomato whenever she visited him in prison. He'd give her money and a bogus weather report, like "Snow showers in New Orleans," and then she'd repeat it to Mr. O'Shaughnessy. She claimed she had no idea what the arrangement was about—who knows what those weather reports really meant—she just took the money and didn't ask questions. Hey, she didn't have a job, and a girl has to survive somehow, right? The only problem is, Hamburger Heaven closed, so lunch will be observed at Burger Heaven instead, just a block over.

§2:00 P.M.§ *Continue walking tour to Port Authority Bus Terminal, where Holly said good-bye to Doc and told him she wasn't coming back to Texas with him.*

§3:00 P.M.§ *A hot dog on the sidewalk on Park Avenue, where Holly told Paul that she was going to Brazil to* marry José da Silva Pereira instead of staying in New York to be with him. Even after Paul told her he loved her, and sort of asked her to marry him, a proposal that she sort of ignored.

⚜4:00 P.M.⚜ *Return to Tiffany's to browse and to ask the clerk if we can get a Cracker Jack ring engraved, just like Paul and Holly did.*

⚜6:00 P.M.⚜ *Return to individual hotels to change.*

⚜8:30 P.M.⚜ *Dinner at "21" Club, which is where Holly was supposed to be when Doc surprised her at her apartment.* It's still a pretty exclusive restaurant—I had to make the reservation more than three months ago to get in. I told the others to pretend we were in our twenties; I don't know if they'd allow a group of teenagers in.

⚜11:00 P.M.⚜ *Arrive at Ziegfeld Theater on Fifty-fourth Street for a special midnight screening of* Breakfast at Tiffany's.

Sunday

⚜12:00 MIDNIGHT⚜ *Settle into theater chairs and watch the greatest movie in the world unfold before our eyes.*

⚜6:00 A.M.⚜ *Reconvene at Tiffany's for another breakfast. Decide whether to stay in New York forever, and if not, why not?*

y toes are pinched in my low black pumps, which almost fit but not quite. I take short steps, a delicate ballet shuffle across the sidewalk, like Audrey did. Back and forth, avoiding the windows. She floated. I don't. I should have practiced a little more.

It took forever to do my hair this morning. I'm not exaggerating. I woke myself up at 4:00 A.M. to do it. Well, 4:09, actually. There must be two dozen bobby pins in there. The shared bathroom at the hotel was flammable with Aqua Net by the time I was finished. I used it to weld the diamond tiara to my updo. I wonder if I'll ever get it out.

I wonder how Audrey got her hairdo that way. I wonder how many hours it took. But then again, she just had to sit there, probably, while a team of fourteen people fawned over her, looking at her from all angles and telling her how beautiful she was, over and over again. Maybe that would suck, too, getting poked at and prodded and having your hair pulled and having people tell you to close your eyes while they spray you with whatever toxic substance kept wayward hairs in place back then. But then again, when you're Audrey Hepburn, a.k.a. the most glamorous movie star of all time, I'm sure everything sucks a little bit less than if you're just, I don't know, me.

I know what you're thinking. You're thinking I'm deluded. Me? Gemma Beasley? Wearing diamonds? Come off it. Gemma Beasley isn't diamonds material.

Well, I'm not deluded. I know they aren't real diamonds. There's no way I, age sixteen, with exactly $140 and a round-trip train ticket from Philadelphia to New York City, can afford a diamond tiara. The best someone like me can do is a crown of plastic rhinestones.

But if you look at it a certain way, the plastic rhinestones are just right. You think Holly Golightly could afford real diamonds on her own? Not a chance. She had to rely on the, well, kindness of others to get her jewels.

There's no one else on the sidewalk. Hardly any cars on Fifth Avenue. This is only my second time in New York but even I know that's weird in this city, even at this perfect hour. But still, I'm startled at the voice, low and insistent, that cuts through the faint mist.

"Need a ride?"

I spin around, nearly dropping my deli bag. A shiny yellow taxi, one of those fancy new electric ones that surprises you because it doesn't make a sound, is crawling around the corner of Fifty-seventh Street like a cat slinking through a backyard after a bird. The driver, a dark-haired guy much younger than I'd expect a taxi driver to be, nods at me.

I clear my throat. "No, thank you, darling," I say, only I try to pronounce it more like *dah-ling*, because that's how Audrey would have said it, with an accent that isn't exactly British but isn't exactly American, either. It's sort of somewhere in between. It took me weeks of practice, recording myself with my iPhone and playing it back again, before I got it down, and even now I still don't really have it exactly right. I make a mental note to move to Holland someday, which is where Audrey grew up, mostly. She was born in Belgium and went to school in London some, too. I've spent my entire life in Philadelphia. But maybe if I get to Holland one day, and I listen to Dutch people speaking English, I'll get Audrey's accent right.

"You sure?" the driver asks.

"I'm already exactly where I need to be," I tell him, and I wave him on, my opera-gloved hand swirling through the air, all glamour and nonchalance.

Nonchalance. That's such an Audrey word.

If you've never waved a taxi away down Fifth Avenue with an opera-gloved hand, nonchalantly, I recommend trying it sometime. Just saying.

5:20 A.M.

I remember the first time I saw Audrey Hepburn. Or, I mean, a picture of Audrey, since she died before I was born.

I was thirteen, and I came home from doing the grocery shopping with a copy of *Teen Vogue*. I tried to hide it from my mother because she always got annoyed whenever I bought anything that wasn't on the list, but she found out about it when she scrutinized the receipt.

"A fashion magazine," she said, shaking her head. "Gemma, you know we can't afford that."

"We can't afford anything anymore," I said, and as soon

as I said it I felt my stomach drop. Mom hated talking about money. Ever since we lost the big house and had to move into the tiny little apartment, which didn't even have a bedroom for me, it was the one subject that I was never allowed to bring up.

I pulled out the shoe box that I kept under the couch. There was an envelope in there, a wrinkled one that stuck shut whenever it was a humid day. I pulled out three dollars from the stack of ones that Gram had given me for my birthday and gave them to her.

"Oh, Gemma," Mom said, and I could hear her voice catch. "Is this really what you want to spend your money on?"

I nodded.

"Sometimes I just don't understand you," she said, folding the money into her wallet. "When are you going to figure out who you really are?"

Later that same evening, after a silent dinner of frozen tofu potpies, and after Mom and Dad went down to the Lancer Lounge for their nightly round (or two) of manhattans, I sat on the floor in our cramped living room and looked at the pictures in *Teen Vogue*. It was the first time in a long while that I had a brand-new magazine, and I loved the smell of it. Usually the magazines I read at the library were already wrinkled and torn. But this one was fresh, with stiff, glossy pages and no smudges.

There were pages and pages of swimsuits ("for all body types"—if your body type was skinny), purses ("for all occasions"—as if I had occasions), and beautiful models posing with perfect, shirtless Abercrombie-esque boys. There were reviews of nail polishes (and removers), a profile of Elle Fanning, party pictures from the Grammys showing Rihanna and Katy Perry pretending to make out, a quiz—"Do You Know How to Say No?"

The main fashion spread was a countdown of the top ten most stylish movie stars of all time, with tips on how you could look like them. It went on for pages. Number 10 was Angelina Jolie in a slim suit, next to a model in a similar suit from Marc Jacobs (as if). Number 9 was Jennifer Lawrence in suede pants and a T-shirt, next to a model in skinny brown jeans and a $350 T-shirt. Number 8 was Emma Stone in a gingham "picnic dress." (Jeez, I wish someone would invite me to a picnic like that someday.) J-Lo in an over-the-top sequined party dress. (For a party that would require an over-the-top sequined number.) And so on. You get the idea.

On the seventh page of the spread was someone I'd never seen before, a tall, slim woman in an old-fashioned black-and-white photo taken on a deserted street in what looked like New York City. She wore a long, strappy, black evening gown. Hair piled high. Pearls, like three strands or maybe more, draping down her back. A tiara. Sunglasses, too. Big and black and movie-star-ish. She was standing at a building under a sign that said TIFFANY & CO., looking in one of the display windows, with a pastry in her mouth.

What was she looking at?

3. Audrey Hepburn was one of the most famous movie stars of the 20th century, and one of the most stylish. She was known for her simple, youthful, sophisticated look. She was serene but bright. She called herself awkward, saying she had gangly legs and a goofy face, but we disagree. She was simply enchanting.

Enchanting. I remember saying it to myself, over and over, marveling at the word. I could barely turn the page; I was transfixed.

It was a funny feeling. I mean, I'd seen so many pictures of beautiful women in beautiful clothes before. In advertisements. On billboards. On television. In magazines. But this one—this one was different. Was it her posture? Was it the dress? Was it the street, Fifth Avenue in New York City, a place I'd only been on day trips with Mom and Dad when she went to visit her editor and Dad and I got ice creams in Central Park?

Enchanting. I knew immediately that I wanted to be enchanting, too. *Maybe that's who I am, Mom. Maybe I'm enchanting.*

I tore the picture out of the magazine and held it up next to my face in the bathroom mirror. I looked at Audrey, with her perfect posture and flawless skin and elegant updo. I looked at myself, with my droopy eyes and boring haircut and fleshy stomach and a zit nestled in the crease of my nose. I looked back at Audrey. Enchanting Audrey. Droopy Gemma.

I folded up the picture and put it in the shoe box. It's still there. And I still look at it every day. And every time I do, I hear Mom saying: *When are you going to figure out who you really are?*

She died six months ago. Just a week before my sixteenth birthday.

Back on the sidewalk, I feel a flash of fear as it stabs through my stomach—*what if I'm the only one who comes?* What if Trina and Bryan blow me off? I feel conspicuous. Another taxi splashes past. I consider hailing it and catching a bus back to Philly. If I get home before dinnertime, Dad might not even notice I've been gone.

Another flash of fear: Just how big of a freak am I? Standing in front of Tiffany's at dawn in a floor-length black gown?

Seriously. If my classmates from Washington Irving High School in Philadelphia saw me right now, it would only confirm what I'm sure they already think: that I'm a hopeless, boyfriendless, vintage-clothes-wearing loner who's never been to Forever 21 or H&M and therefore knows nothing about fashion or style or how people should dress. They don't know, or care, about things like Christian Dior. Or the difference between "the New Look" and "Mod." Or Charles James or Cristóbal Balenciaga or Pauline Trigère or Diana Vreeland or *Funny Face* or *Roman Holiday* or *Sabrina* or anything else I actually care about, least of all Audrey Hepburn.

"Isn't she the one in *On Golden Pond?*" one girl, a particularly obnoxious one, said once. "My grandmother loves that movie. She forces us to watch it whenever we visit her at Shady Meadows."

"No, that was Katharine Hepburn," I said. "They weren't related."

"Um, whatever? You know, you should try this century out for a change, Gina."

"Gemma. It's Gemma," I said, but the girl was already gone and I was talking to myself, which seems to happen a lot. More than ever now since Mom died and I have one less person to talk to.

Or maybe I've always talked to myself, come to think of it. I remember Mom telling me that I used to talk to my stuffed animals when I was a kid. And sometimes she'd point it out when I was talking to myself over my homework or while I was riding in the car with her.

"Gem?" she'd say. "Are you having one of your imaginary

conversations again?" And she'd laugh, and I'd feel silly but not embarrassed, because she was my mom and she thought my imagination was important.

Since she's been gone, no one really points it out to me anymore. It's my responsibility to notice when I'm talking to myself now.

It's my responsibility for a lot of things, which sucks. It kind of pisses me off sometimes. Did I ask her to die so that I could have more responsibility? Did I ask to be the one to have to take care of the apartment? Did I ask to be the only person who my father talks to anymore? Did I ask for him to text me every twenty minutes, where before just one short conversation a day would be enough? Is it my fault he doesn't have any friends and just sits around the living room reading her books or asking me what I want for dinner or, always hovering, asking me if I need to "talk"?

And you wonder why I ran away.

Or whatever you call this.

Funny how when you're dressed up like Audrey Hepburn and standing outside Tiffany's in New York City, even a siren in the distance can sound like a song. You don't really think that there's probably a tragedy attached to it, like someone dying.

nother taxi, only this one stops across the street. A girl emerges. A young woman, I mean, in a khaki trench coat and matching flats. Trina? Could it be? I start to smile, to raise my arm for a wave. But she doesn't see me. She ducks into the service entrance just a few doors down from the Bulgari jewelry shop.

Not Trina.

They'll come. Of course they'll come. Bryan for sure. He's coming all the way from Beverly Hills, excuse me, *Bel-Air*,

California. And as far as I knew last night, he still hadn't told his parents that he was leaving for New York. "What they don't know won't hurt them," he'd said.

"You're such a rebel," I'd said.

Of course he'll come. *See you tomorrow*, he'd texted last night. *I can't wait.* He's my most reliable friend.

Friend.

Can you call someone you only know from the Internet a friend?

I smooth out my skirt and wonder what my mother would have said about my dress.

I think she would have said it was silly. That my obsession with Audrey Hepburn was superficial. That I shouldn't try to dress like anyone else, or act like anyone else, or talk or walk or dream like anyone else. I'm sure of it.

Who needs Audrey Hepburn when the world has Gemma Beasley?

Of course she would say that. Moms say those kinds of things to their kids all the time even though they are totally unrealistic. I guess they're trying to make us feel better about ourselves. But seriously, who would want to be Gemma Beasley instead of Audrey Hepburn? Still, I guess it was kind of nice to hear.

Mom was so smart. Always reading, always writing. So determined to write the "great American novel" or the "great feminist novel" or the great whatever novel, so long as someone somewhere would read it and recognize her for the massive talent she wanted to be. Before the bank took over the farm in the country and we moved to the one-bedroom apartment in Philadelphia, she'd spend hours—days, even—out in her "writing shack," which was really an old barn that my dad had outfitted with bookshelves, a desk, and a woodstove. She used a typewriter. She said it was how all the great novels were written. Computers made things too easy.

"Ideas, Gem," she'd say. "I need ideas! What's in your head today? What's in your imagination?" And I'd tell her: The cats, I thought, spoke in a secret language to one another. My grandmother—was she secretly a sorceress, mixing up love potions in the basement? What if I had a long-lost twin sister living in a sprawling palace on the outskirts of Moscow? Was there a space-age jet pack hidden out in the woods that I could strap on to fly down to the Amazon rain forest and pick exotic flowers for the afternoon?

"Oh, Gem," she'd say, laughing and smiling while I squirmed on her lap, unable to contain my imagination, "you are a natural storyteller. One day you'll grow up and the whole world will hear your stories! Maybe we'll even write a book together! And I will be so proud of my little Gem." And she'd kiss me on the forehead and ask me to tell Dad to start dinner.

"What are we having?" I'd ask.

"What's your favorite?" she'd reply.

"Fried clams!"

"Gemma, I love you so. But where you got your love for seafood I'll never know."

It was true. Mom and Dad couldn't stand seafood, but I loved it. Still do. Lobster, tuna, salmon, mussels, shrimps, even raw oysters. I'm the only one I know who likes those.

Things changed, of course. They always do. After the fore closure, when we moved to the apartment in the city and my mother started working at the thrift shop for minimum wage, she stopped asking me about my imagination. She'd scowl when I'd try to tell her the stories I'd made up. She'd shake her head, tired, and tell me I was just being foolish. "Don't waste your time on stories," she'd say. "They won't pay the rent." Then she'd tell Dad to take her down to the Lancer Lounge. "I need a drink," she'd say. "I'm not happy."

Who knows if she was already sick by then? I didn't, and I don't think Dad did, either. I'm not even sure that she did. But one night, just a week before my sixteenth birthday, she threw up blood after coming home from the Lancer Lounge.

· · · · ·

Like I said, things change.

I pull my smartphone out of my clutch and bring up Trina's
e-mail from last night.

Subject: You were right.

*And not just you, Gemma. Everyone was right. Miles is a beast. A
rat. I would elaborate if even thinking about him didn't make me
sick to my stomach. What I need is a grown-up. You know, a man
who will give a girl $50 to go to the powder room. Lol.*

*Do say you'll forgive me for neglecting the Tumblr lately. I've
been so busy, darling, working double shifts to save up for New
York. Do say you'll forgive me, do.*

I can't wait to get out of here, Gemma. I just don't belong here.

All love, dahling,

Trina

Bad news, but the e-mail makes me smile. I wonder if she
talks like that in real life. Like, at work at the restaurant. Can
you imagine? "Would you like a side salad, *dah-ling?*" Or, "Do
try the shrimp special. *Do.*" She almost sounds sarcastic, but
I know she's not. At least I think she's not. Maybe it depends
on who she's talking to.

Fifty dollars for the powder room. That's what Holly

Golightly did. Or at least that's what she said. The men she went out with gave her fifty dollars for the powder room. I remember reading on some website someplace about how hanging out with rich men who gave her fifty dollars for the powder room pretty much made Holly Golightly a prostitute, but I don't see it that way. Holly was just a smart, resourceful girl, one who managed to put herself into situations where rich men would give her money for things as simple as going to the powder room. It's not like she asked them for money. I think they just gave it to her for her companionship. For how she made them feel just being by her side—fabulous. Important. *Enchanting*, like her.

Besides, what was she supposed to do, say no? She needed the money. She was on her own. Everyone needs money.

Which I can totally relate to. Needing money, that is. Things have been pretty tough since Mom died. I picked up some of her old shifts at the thrift store to help Dad out. They pay me in cash, seven dollars an hour, which I keep in my shoe box. How else could I afford this trip? Besides, I don't think any rich Brazilians like José da Silva Pereira are in my future.

wave away another cab. I guess there aren't a lot of people out this morning. You always hear about how the competition for taxis in New York is so fierce, but here I am waving them away.

Still twenty-five minutes until my friends get here.

It's funny how I talk about Trina and Bryan like I know them, because I don't. Not unless you count being Facebook friends and e-mailing one another and texting and talking on the phone and on Skype and sharing a Tumblr page as "knowing" one another. But I do.

I guess I feel closer to them than I do to anyone in my so-called real life.

Our Tumblr page is called *Oh, Yeah, Audrey!* Actually, if you want to get technical, it was really *my* Tumblr page before they joined in. I started it after Mom died, mostly as a place for me to post pictures of Audrey Hepburn. I didn't really know if anyone else would ever see it or not. Which no one did, at first. I put up a new picture every single day, though—Audrey in a striped sailor's shirt, Audrey on a Vespa, Audrey at the Oscars, Audrey in a cowboy hat.

I showed the Tumblr page to Dad right after I launched it.

"How much does it cost?" he said.

"It's free," I said. "Don't worry."

"I don't get it," he said. "What's the point?"

"It's like a library of pictures," I said.

"Libraries have a point," Dad said. "They help people. How is this little obsession of yours ever going to help anyone?"

"I don't know," I said. *But it helps me.*

"Don't you have homework to do? Biology, maybe?"

"Don't worry," I said. "I'll get all A's. I always do."

"That's my girl," he said.

But I had my doubts.

I posted new pictures to the Tumblr page every day, without fail. Sometimes two a day, or three. It's not that hard to find pictures of Audrey Hepburn on the Internet. You should try it.

Anyway, I met Trina, if you can call it "meeting" her, when

she first made a comment on *Oh Yeah, Audrey!* It surprised me because, like I said, I didn't think anyone ever looked at it. Underneath a photo of Audrey in pretty much the same strappy black dress I'm wearing now, she wrote: *Thank you, dahling, for not calling the above picture a little black dress like everyone always does. That dress is hardly little. Audrey doesn't wear a little black dress until she goes to Sing Sing to visit Sally Tomato!*

I responded: *Who are you and why are you living in my head?*

Obviously, Trina doesn't actually live in my head. Trina Belen lives in Denver, Colorado, which is a place I don't know anything about, but who cares? She doesn't know anything about Philadelphia, either, and we talk mostly about Audrey Hepburn anyway, which is totally fine by me because it's pretty much all I ever want to talk about these days. We've seen all of her movies, or at least clips. They're all over YouTube. Talking to Trina about Audrey Hepburn is like talking to myself, only not exactly. She knows all the same things I do, but she doesn't always see them the same way. Like, Holly Golightly insists on calling Paul Varjak, her handsome upstairs neighbor, Fred. Holly tells Paul she wants to call him Fred because he reminds her of her brother in the army, whose name really *is* Fred. Trina just doesn't understand why Holly would do that. But to me it makes perfect sense.

"She misses him," I told her.

"Whatever. I miss my brother in Afghanistan. But I don't call other people Timmy just because Timmy's not around."

Just last month she told me he's been gone for three years. "I barely even know him anymore," she said. "Of course, he's all my parents can talk about. Tim this and Tim that. They don't even call him Timmy anymore, the way they used to. But the way they talk about him, like he's some kind of god or something, it's like they're talking about someone else."

"He's still your brother, Trina."

"Whatever. It's like nothing I do will ever be as great as what he's doing. I work all the time, too, busting my butt at the restaurant. Does anyone notice that? No."

"That sucks," I said.

"Well, I can't expect them to notice. It's not like they aren't working sixty-hour weeks waiting tables, too. It's a family curse, I guess."

"All of you?"

"Yep. Me, my sister, and my parents. Not at the same restaurant, though. Or I should say restaurants. Mom and Dad each have two jobs. No one will give them a full-time schedule so they pick up shifts from two different places. Each."

"Wow," I said.

"It sucks," she said. Then, after a pause, "I bet I won't even recognize him when he comes home. *If* he comes home."

"Who?"

"My brother," she said.

"Trina, don't say that."

"Whatever. I'll be out of here soon." She paused a moment. "And until then, I'm not going to go around calling my friends by my brother's name," she said. "I think it's just weird. *Dahling*."

I laughed. Trina cracks me up. She's half-dainty, all *dahling* this and *dahling* that, and half-tough. She doesn't hold back her opinion. Like two opposite people in one. But I like them both and, besides, who isn't at least two opposite people in one? Sometimes I feel like four or five people during the course of a day.

I gave her the password so she could start posting pictures of Audrey Hepburn, too.

"So tell me about *your* parents," she asked. "All you ever do is listen to me complain about mine!"

Sometimes I wanted to tell her. I really wanted to open my mouth, or start typing away on the keyboard, and let everything I felt about my dead mom and depressed dad come flowing out of me. Like if I just spilled it all, everything would be better and I'd feel lighter. But I never knew exactly what to say or how to start. What's the first word to use when you tell someone that your mother died? So I'd usually just turn the conversation back to her and get her started on another funny story. It was just easier that way.

• • • • •

A pool of cool air bursts up the sidewalk, and I hunch my shoulders. A glint of light reflects off the windows of the Louis Vuitton store across the street, sending beams of white-pink light onto the sidewalk, where they dance around my slippers.

I grasp my coffee tighter, looking for warmth, but I can feel it getting cold in my hand. I don't pop the lid and take a sip. Not yet.

ryan found the Tumblr page at around the same time as Trina. He posted a picture of Audrey lying by a pool, a really glamorous pool with palm trees just behind it. *Here she is in 1954, in the pool at the house right across the street from me, when Lauren Bacall lived there.*

Bryan Akito from Bel-Air, in Los Angeles, California. He doesn't ever brag about how rich he is, but he doesn't ignore it, either. "I live in a mansion. My neighbors are Will Smith and Chelsea Handler. I got a Mercedes for my seventeenth birthday. I took horseback-riding lessons on our ranch in Santa Barbara. What can I say?"

His parents are television producers. They made millions off some science fiction series in the 1990s. I forget which one, something about a high-tech colony marooned on a space station that had to fight off a different kind of alien in each episode. Not really my kind of show.

"Mine, either," Bryan said once. "The only way I'd watch a sci-fi movie is if it had Barbara Stanwyck in it."

I couldn't believe it. I couldn't believe anyone else had ever even heard of Barbara Stanwyck. But Bryan knows everything about old movies. Everything. He knows the difference between Betty Grable and Betty Bacall, between Gary Cooper and Cary Grant. He can recite *All About Eve* the whole way through, line for line, and he can tell you what color dress Rita Hayworth was wearing in the nightclub scene in *Gilda* even though it's a black-and-white movie. He can describe exactly every set in *Auntie Mame*, down to the cocktail cart. He can recite Elizabeth Taylor's full name, accounting for all eight of her marriages: *Elizabeth Taylor Hilton Wilding Todd Fisher Burton Burton Warner Fortensky*. He can sketch every outfit Grace Kelly wore in *To Catch a Thief* and her hairstyles, too. He can strike every pose Joan Crawford did in *Mildred Pierce*. He knows which of Bette Davis's gowns were designed by Edith Head and which were designed by Adrian, although Bryan says Edith Head's designs were better almost every time. He even knows Marilyn Monroe's measurements by heart. "I use them as my PIN number."

But Audrey Hepburn is his favorite. Of course.

"Audrey Hepburn is the greatest movie star of all time," he said to me once. "The ultimate. Exquisite. Perfection. She wasn't the greatest actor or the most successful or the greatest beauty. But she was perfect. There was never any movie star like her before her, and there will never be anyone like her again. Ever. Period."

I love the way Bryan talks in absolutes. He never says things like "in my opinion" or "I think"; he just says, "Audrey Hepburn is the greatest movie star of all time." Like it's a fact.

Sometimes I wonder whether Bryan has any friends in Bel-Air. He never talks about his social life. Well, that's not totally true. There's that one time, a couple months ago, that he told me he had to get some stitches removed from his forehead.

I asked, "Stitches? From what?"

"You know how it is, Gemma," he told me.

"What happened?"

"Nothing, really, just some guys from school," he said.

"What do you mean?" I asked.

"Look, remember last week when I mentioned I'd gotten

these great new Thom Browne pants, midcalf, and the bright orange Cole Haan oxfords?"

"Yeah! You sent me a pic. So cute."

"And remember how I told you they were really women's oxfords because they didn't make men's oxfords in that exact color?"

"So what?" I said. It's not like the shoes are any different. "I buy guys' shoes all the time, you know."

"Those oxfords didn't survive the day, Gemma. And neither did my forehead." He paused a moment before going on. "There's this jerk who's constantly harassing me at school. He's a complete meathead. You know the type. Can't really form a sentence but still seems to have tons of friends around all the time? Anyway, he came up to me in the stairwell and asked me where I got my quote-unquote fabulous shoes. He pointed them out to the five other guys who were standing there, too. 'Aren't they *fabulous*?' he said. I didn't answer, of course, because he's not the kind of person to use the word *fabulous* unless he's up to something. Anyway, he pretended to bend over for a closer look and quote-unquote accidentally spilled his Powerade all over them."

"Bryan."

"So of course, being an idiot, I bent down to wipe it off. Well, let's just say you shouldn't bend down to wipe off stains at the top of a staircase in front of six guys you know hate you."

"I'm so sorry," I said. "I wish I'd been there. I'd have pushed them all down the stairs and watched them pile up into a heap at the bottom."

"That would have been awesome," he said. "Except they would have landed on me."

We both cracked up. When we were done, we were silent for a moment. Then Bryan spoke.

"I just can't wait to get out of here," he said.

"I know the feeling," I said.

"What do you mean?" he asked.

"I just—" And then I didn't know what to say. It was like my breath caught in my throat and I felt this wave come over me, like maybe I'd cry.

"Gemma?"

"Nothing," I said.

"I don't believe you," he said. "Something's wrong."

"I'm OK," I said.

"Of course you are. That doesn't mean nothing's wrong. I can tell. This will sound really weird, but it's like I can see you. I know I'm in California and you're in Philadelphia, but I can see you."

"That's crazy," I said.

"I know. But, Gemma, if you ever want to talk . . ."

"About what?" I said.

"About anything. You know that, right?"

I did. I knew it. But I couldn't get the words *I know* out without my voice cracking. "Thanks" was all I said, and then I changed the subject to the Oscars, which were coming up in a couple of weeks.

I see a young guy in a suit walking up Fifth Avenue toward me. Is it him? He strides closer, talking on his phone, before stepping off the curb and crossing the street. I can see his trousers are too long, bunching at the hems.

It's not Bryan. He'd never wear his pants that way.

5:45 A.M.

*I*f I "know" Trina and Bryan, I guess that means I know Telly, too. Not that I really want to. Not after all the horrible comments she's made on *Oh Yeah, Audrey!* If *she* even is a she. You never really know on the Internet. For all I know, "Telly" is a lumberjack from the Northwest Territories.

The person who calls himself/herself Telly found *Oh Yeah, Audrey!* a few months ago. The first comment she posted was underneath a beautiful picture of Audrey Hepburn lying on the floor in a black turtleneck and black cigarette pants, propped up on her elbows with her long legs stretched out behind her. *Big deal. I could starve myself and look like that, too,* he/she wrote.

After that, she never stopped posting. She was always complaining about how skinny Audrey was. *Starvation chic,* she'd write, or *Emaciated,* or *I bet she was on drugs,* or *Somebody give her a sandwich.*

Once, she even posted a link to her own Facebook page, where she'd put up a screenshot of Audrey Hepburn as Holly Golightly in the belted trench coat she wore in the final scene of *Breakfast at Tiffany's* when she goes looking for the cat named Cat in a back alley during a rainstorm. Only, on Telly's Facebook page, the picture had been blown up in Photoshop to make Audrey look really, really fat. Like, *really* fat.

That's more like it was the accompanying comment. (For the record, it only had two "likes," and I have a feeling they were both from Telly herself.)

Her comments made Bryan really mad, because for one thing, Audrey was beautiful (or to be more precise, "the most beautiful creature who ever lived and anyone who doesn't agree just doesn't know what they're talking about"), and for another thing, Audrey didn't choose to be so skinny. She just was skinny. In fact, Bryan said that he'd read in a biography about her that when she was a child during World War II, she had to hide from the Nazis in a basement in Holland. For a month. A month! Kind of like in *The Diary of Anne Frank*, only Audrey was in a basement instead of an attic. Bryan said that some producers in Hollywood tried to get her to play Anne Frank in the movie but Audrey said no way. It was too close to home for her and, besides, she was in her twenties when they asked and shouldn't a teenager play the part? Anyway, Bryan said that her metabolism was never really the same after that experience, and she always had a hard time eating and putting on weight.

And don't even ask what Trina thinks about Telly. I'll paraphrase: "Does she have a neck? If so, I look forward to wringing it."

Personally, I find Telly totally annoying, but there's a part of me that also wonders what kind of person would be so committed to bringing someone like Audrey Hepburn down. Either she's just plain evil or she's totally insecure and hates herself. Maybe both. I feel sorry for whoever this Telly is. Maybe she's trying to put down Audrey because her life sucks, too. Like Trina's. Like Bryan's. Like mine.

Telly knows about the *Breakfast at Tiffany's* meeting. Anyone who follows *Oh Yeah, Audrey!* knows about it. Everyone's invited. But only Bryan and Trina have said they will show up.

I can't wait for midnight.

They say the Ziegfeld Theater has one of the biggest movie screens anywhere, and soon I will see Audrey Hepburn sashay across it. So far, even though I've watched *Breakfast at Tiffany's* around one million times, I've only ever seen it on a small television screen and on the laptop Dad got us after . . . you know.

I straighten my pearls (fake, obvs). I tell myself that even if six o'clock comes and goes and I'm still alone on the sidewalk, my breakfast at Tiffany's will still be perfect. Holly had her breakfast alone. So can I.

Maybe it'd be better that way anyway.

he misty air has left a sparkly sheen on the pavement, and the street glistens as the sky gets brighter. Still no one else here. Not Bryan, not Trina, not Telly. Not even Dusty.

Have I mentioned Dusty? Dusty-haired Dusty with the slate-gray eyes? I wonder if he's coming. Yesterday I hoped so. Today I hope not.

I don't know.

A town car lumbers by, followed by a school bus, crawling slowly downtown.

A school bus? In New York City? I wonder what school it

belongs to. I wonder if it's Dusty's school. His fancy private school on the Upper East Side. I wonder what it's like there, with all those rich kids in expensive clothes. I wonder if it's like *Gossip Girl*. I wonder how many beautiful girls are there, how many of them Dusty likes. How many of them Dusty has dated. Is dating.

I wonder what he really means when he says stuff like "You seem really cool," or "Do you have a boyfriend?"

I know what you're thinking. You think I have a crush on Dusty. But I don't. How could I have a crush on someone I've never met in person?

Dusty follows the *Oh Yeah, Audrey!* page also, but not for the same reasons the rest of us do. He's not obsessed with Audrey Hepburn or anything like that.

He first posted a note on the page a few weeks ago, asking for help on a school report he was working on. Something about Hubert de Givenchy, the one who designed all of Holly Golightly's dresses. "It's my punishment for skipping film class," he wrote. "Three days in a row." He said that he needed help figuring out which dresses to include in his report. "Can you help me pick? I don't know anything about this stuff."

I heard my dad's voice. *How is this little obsession of yours ever going to help anyone?*

"I'm going to help him," I told Trina later on the phone. "Why not? It's like being a Good Samaritan."

"Save the world, Gemma," Trina said.

I sent Dusty a dozen pictures of Audrey Hepburn for his report. He said thanks. I said you're welcome. He asked me questions about her, like where she was from and how old she was and stuff, and I answered. Born in Belgium, but lived in England, Amsterdam, Los Angeles, and Switzerland. She would be eighty-four now, but she died in 1993, when she was sixty-three. Cancer. She was twenty-four when she won an Oscar for *Roman Holiday*. Thirty-one when she made *Breakfast at Tiffany's*. She was on everyone's Best Dressed list. She always wore clothes by the designer Hubert de Givenchy, even when the movie she was working on had a different costume person.

"Didn't that piss off the costume person?" Dusty asked.

"Probably," I answered. "But it was part of her contract."

"Thanks," he said. "I really appreciate this."

It felt good to be helpful. Even in a non-saving-the-world way.

"You're welcome," I wrote.

Later that night, Bryan e-mailed me and Trina. "Anyone else look him up on Facebook? He's beyond cute. There's a picture of him on a yacht. No shirt. Great smile. Cute sneakers. Pecs. That little vein running down his biceps. Yum."

"A yacht?" Trina wrote back. "Is he rich?"

"I'm sure," I wrote.

"What!?" Trina wrote. "A girl needs to know these things!

I mean, is he the kind of guy who gives a girl fifty dollars for the powder room?" That was from *Breakfast at Tiffany's*.

"We know what Holly Golightly is *really* doing in that powder room for fifty dollars!" Bryan joked.

"As if!" I scolded him. "Holly gets fifty dollars for being her fabulous self. And that's the end of it!" I exclaimed.

"Gemma Beasley, I love Holly just as much as you do, but it takes more than being fabulous for men to throw money at you. *You* need a reality check."

But that was the thing. Who wants a reality check when you can be having breakfast at Tiffany's?

"Anyway," Bryan continued, "Dusty's dad is Jimmy Sant'Angelo, the music producer. You know, the guy who produces all those rap stars. Do you know how rich that guy is? Crazy rich."

"Out of my league," Trina wrote. "Whatever. He's probably a jerk. All those rich bros are. *Quel rat*." Another line borrowed from *Breakfast*.

I'll admit that I thought Dusty looked cute, and those biceps were—well, I noticed them. And he was obviously incredibly rich. But those weren't the reasons I decided to help him. There's something about someone asking for help with something that you know about that makes you just want to help. You know what I mean? I'd asked people questions on the Internet before and been totally ignored, and it sucked. I didn't want to be that person. Besides, it was no big deal. It's not like I didn't have hundreds of pictures of Audrey Hepburn to share.

Dusty asked if he could call me to ask me more questions. "I really need to ace this paper. I need to graduate on time. Can I have your number?"

I told him no, but that I would call him. I blocked my number before I did it. I may be helpful, but I'm not stupid. I've seen those shows about what happens to people who share their numbers with strangers. You never really know who's out there on the Internet. Ax murderers, for example.

"Hello?" Dusty's voice was sleepy when he answered, like he'd just woken up.

"Is this a bad time?" I asked.

"No," he said, and I think I heard him yawn. "It's perfect."

We talked for an hour about Audrey Hepburn. Or more like, I talked and he listened. I could hear him typing in the background. I told him just about everything I know about her movies and her fashion and everything else. I explained what cigarette pants are and why they're called that, and what the difference is between an A-line skirt and a pencil skirt, and what slingbacks are, and mules, and kitten heels. I explained why you call it a tiara and not a crown, why long dresses have slits, and why women love to dress in black.

"How do you know all this stuff?" he asked.

"I just know it, I guess," I said.

"No, seriously, you're really smart."

"I'm not that smart," I said.

"Yeah. You are," he said.

I didn't answer. I just sat there with my phone to my ear, blushing.

That's right. I was alone, at home, on the couch with my laptop and phone, talking with someone I didn't know, and I blushed.

"Hello?" he said.

"Sorry."

"I thought you'd gone."

"Nopc," I said.

"So people really think Audrey Hepburn was beautiful, huh?"

"Oh, yes," I said, breathing again. "One of the most beautiful ever. Don't you?"

"I suppose she's cute," he said.

"But?"

"But she's not really my type."

I paused.

"What is your type?"

No answer.

"I mean . . . ," I said.

"What type are you?" he asked.

didn't tell Bryan and Trina about that first phone call with Dusty. Or the second one, or the third. And if you asked me right now, I don't know if I even remember what we talked about during all those phone calls. Have you ever just found yourself so relaxed on the phone that you forget you're actually talking to someone else, and it just feels like you're talking to yourself? Not like talking to a brick wall, but just going through your head and finding things that feel like they need to be said so you say them, and then before you know it you're just talking.

Just a few nights ago, we were talking about—I don't even remember—when my father interrupted us.

"Gemma!" he yelled from the doorway. He was just getting home from work.

I covered the phone with my hand. "I'm on the phone!"

"Hang up! I need you!"

"I'm busy!"

"What could be so important? Just hang up!"

"In a minute!" I spoke into the phone again. "Sorry."

"Who was that?" Dusty asked.

"My dad," I said. "He's driving me so crazy lately. He's totally on my case and I don't know why. It's like he doesn't care what *I* want to do, where *I* want to go. And he never wants to leave me alone. I mean, I'm a sixteen-year-old girl. I can't spend all of my time with my dad, you know? It's been that way ever since Mom . . ."

I stopped myself.

I hadn't talked to Dusty about my mother. I hadn't wanted to. Maybe that was why he and I always had such an easy time talking to each other. Everyone else in my life, as soon as they found out that my mother was dead, would freak out. They'd treat me differently, like I had some kind of disease or something.

"What about your mom?"

"Whatever. It doesn't matter."

"Yes, it does," Dusty said. "It matters. You matter, Gem."

I didn't say anything. I just held my breath for a moment. I didn't want to start to cry. Holding my breath is my most reliable technique for that. I don't know why I wanted to cry just then. No one had called me Gem since Mom. And *You matter* isn't really the kind of thing you hear every day when you're Gemma Beasley.

"Are you there?"

I let my breath go. "I'm sorry," I whispered. "She's dead. A few months ago. Cancer."

At first, Dusty didn't say anything, and I braced myself for what always happens when people find out that your mother's dead.

I noticed it right after she was gone. Even at the funeral. People look at you funny, with these sad eyes, like they're trying to look like they *understand*. As if.

They try to come up with words that will have it make sense. It's like I can hear their brains turning over in their heads, like a computer trying to reboot, whirring and clicking. *I'm so sorry,* they say, as if it's their fault. Or, *I can imagine how hard that must be.* Or, *It's so good you can be there for your father.* Or, the very worst, *At least she's in a better place now.*

They say things that people have always said about things

like dead mothers. They become actors, trying to remember whatever line sounds right.

Only, none of the words ever sound right. There are no words that can. I mean, it's not your fault she's dead, so why would you say you're *so sorry*? And no, you can't imagine *how hard it must be*. Honestly, I don't want to have to *be there for my father*. And no, frankly, she's not *in a better place now*. She's in the ground. You really think that's better?

But those are the words people say to you when they find out that your mother's dead. It's like the news knocks them out of being themselves and into being someone else. Someone they think they're supposed to be instead of someone they really are.

It's the first step in distancing themselves, in getting away from you. Like you're contagious or something, or they just don't want to deal with you anymore.

I guess it's why I never told Trina and Bryan. I never really wanted them to know. I didn't want them to start saying things they didn't mean, just because they thought they should.

But I took a chance with Dusty. And all Dusty Sant'Angelo said was, "That sucks."

Just as easy as could be: "That sucks."

It was the best answer he could have given.

"Thanks," I said.

"For what?"

"Nothing."

Which was kind of a lie, because I was thanking him for something. Something major.

This person who I didn't know, this person who I had never met and probably had nothing in common with, who knew nothing about me, this person—this *boy*—just did the only thing I ever wanted anyone to do. He just said, "That sucks," and that's it. Just like I'm a normal person. A regular girl who happens to have a huge Audrey Hepburn obsession and a dead mother. Somehow—through the phone, the Internet, the atmosphere—he understood me. Just plain me. And he didn't freak out.

Later that night, he e-mailed me a playlist. Four different renditions of "Moon River," including the one that Audrey Hepburn sang on the fire escape in *Breakfast at Tiffany's*. I listened to all four of them twice. I thought maybe I'd cry, but I didn't.

Later, I went back and looked at those pictures on his Facebook page. The ones on the yacht. I hadn't noticed it the first time, but he looked just like George Peppard, a.k.a. Paul Varjak, a.k.a. "Fred," from *Breakfast at Tiffany's*.

ow did I miss that it's past six?

The traffic is picking up and I'm looking less and less *enchanting* and more and more weird, standing here outside Tiffany's in my Audrey Hepburn getup. Then again, I wonder if anyone will even notice. I mean, I guess it's not that weird for New York City. The bar is pretty high for weird here. I'm sure I'm not the first girl to stand out in front of Tiffany's in a strappy black gown at dawn, waiting.

Waiting.

Waiting.

The sidewalk is filling up now. Women in business suits. Men in workout shorts. Students with backpacks, texting as they walk. But no Bryan. No Trina.

I don't know why I thought they'd actually come. I shouldn't be surprised. I guess I don't really know them at all. I've decided having friends just sets you up for more disappointment.

Whatever, I'll have my breakfast at Tiffany's alone. It was good enough for Holly.

I open my deli bag and pop a pastry between my teeth, just like she did. I hold it there while I peel the lid off my paper coffee cup, just like she did. The coffee's lukewarm now. *I bet hers was, too*, I think.

I drop the lid back into the bag and turn toward Tiffany's.

"Hey, sweetheart, do you mind?"

I spin around to see an old man with lopsided glasses and a wrinkly sweatshirt and hair coming out of his ears. He's pointing at my foot, which is being sniffed by a tiny little dog with a tiny little rhinestone collar. White, puffy, with mean eyes. *Really* mean eyes. And teeth, white and sharp and on full display. *Growl. Yap.* I feel the leash wrapping around my ankle.

The man sighs. "Gladiator always walks along the edge of this building," he's saying. "Right along here. *Every* morning." He says it like it's something I'm supposed to know. Like everyone knows this is where Gladiator walks every morning.

"I'm sorry, sir." I pull off my sunglasses and step out of the leash, spilling lukewarm coffee on my shoes just as Gladiator lifts his tiny, fuzzy little leg just inches from my pump.

"Close call," I say, smiling at the man, who is now mumbling in a different direction. The romance of this moment—I've imagined it so many times—is beginning to fade. I mean, a bichon frise named Gladiator just about peed on my pump.

"Excuse me!" a jogger yells from behind me. She clips my left arm and sends my sunglasses flying into a shallow puddle. "Sorry," she breathes, but she doesn't sound like she means it. She trots off, yoga pants tight across her butt.

I bend down to pick up my glasses, shaking the dirty water off them as I stand back up.

Enough. I'm out of here.

I nearly stumble to keep from stepping on the toes parked in front of me. I start to lose my balance, falling forward, but I can't take my eyes off the wingtips. Such a beautiful cognac color. So softly shined.

"Leaving already, Audrey?" he says, catching me by the elbow.

"Huh?"

"It's only six fifteen. Don't you know that, in New York, 'on time' means fifteen minutes late? It's some kind of rule, I think."

Bryan.

I look up from the shoes, the mesmerizing shoes, past the trim trousers, to the skinny purple tie, to the slim jacket. *That suit.* Just like Paul's, in *Breakfast at Tiffany's.* Springtime gray, tailored to just graze the tops of the cognac wingtips.

"Hello, Gemma," he says.

"Hi," I say. Stupid, I know, but it's all I could come up with. Here I'd been maintaining perfect posture all morning, my cape draped just right, my sunglasses perfectly placed—and Bryan appears when I'm tripping over my own feet, dripping sunglasses hanging from one hand. "I'm sorry."

"For what?" he says. "You're perfect."

His eyes are darker than I expected. Deep brown, with flecks of chestnut. His black hair, so precisely parted and carefully combed, shines. He's tall, taller than I am anyway, which maybe isn't that tall really, but it's tall enough. Lean. His voice is deeper than the one I'm accustomed to on the phone. "I meant to be here on time," he says. "But I had a slow start."

He raises one eyebrow, perfectly, like he's practiced it, like a movie star. An old Hollywood movie star, like Cary Grant. Montgomery Clift. Clark Gable. I devolve into a goofy smile and look at my feet.

"You're right on time," I say.

"Take a look at you," he says, and he strokes his chin with his thumb and forefinger. As though he has a beard, which he doesn't. I feel his eyes inspect every stitch and hem and drape. Scrutinizing. Studying. Appreciating?

"Give me a turn," he commands.

I spin, holding up my skirt with my thumb and forefinger. Will he approve?

Bryan smiles, first with his eyes, and then with his lips. He claps, just once. "Givenchy?" he asks. "Tell me it's real!"

"As far as you know," I say.

He steps back. "You look just like . . ."

"Don't say it."

"Just like *her*."

"Stop," I say. I fan myself in mock bashfulness. "And what about you, Bryan?" I chew on the arm of my sunglasses, doing my best Audrey. "You look just like Fred. Paul, I mean! Varjak, Paul! Charming. Positively . . . *rakish*. New suit?"

"You think I wear wool gabardine in Bel-Air?"

Of course it's a new suit. This is Bryan. He can afford it. He can afford just about anything, as far as I can tell.

"I'm glad you're here," I say. I really am.

He kisses my forehead. "Anyone else?" He looks up and down Fifth Avenue. "Trina?"

"No."

"Ah." He nods his head, then smiles again. "This is more than enough for me."

"Pastry?" I hold open the white deli bag.

He takes a croissant and bites off the end. "Breakfast at Tiffany's," he says. He holds out his arm, I crook mine around his, and together we walk over to the window.

"Must be at least fifty or a hundred carats altogether," Bryan says, pointing at an elaborate wrist cuff. "That center-piece stone, that's easily six or seven carats alone. And the smaller ones, they must be a half carat each, and they go all around the wrist. Three strands. Amazing."

"How much?" I say.

"Half mil at least," he says.

"Are you kidding?"

"Hardly. My dad got a tennis bracelet from Tiffany's for my mom last year when she turned forty," Bryan says. "He told me he spent two hundred on it, and that was only one strand, with no centerpiece stone."

"Wow" is all I can say. I don't even understand what numbers like that mean. A half million dollars? Isn't that, like, a couple of houses?

I look into the window and think how perfect everything inside is. Everything is so beautiful. Everything is right where it belongs.

"They're so beautiful," I say.

"So are you," Bryan says.

A flash lights up the window. And another. A camera.

"Tourists," Bryan whispers.

I slide on my sunglasses. We're tourists, too, I'm thinking, but I don't say it out loud. It would ruin the illusion, the illusion that we belong here. That *I* belong here. Just like the diamonds in the window.

"Let's go around the corner," he says after the next flash. "There's another window there." We bow our heads and turn away, giggling.

We get two steps away when a voice stops us. *"Dahlings!"*

I look up. Of course it's Trina, in a dress exactly like mine, except four inches longer because she's four inches taller, at least. She, too, has the big sunglasses and the ivory-colored cape. Her hair is piled high just like mine, only hers is red. Very red. So much redder than it looks in her profile picture. I can't see her eyes yet, because she's holding a camera in front of her face, pointed straight at us. "Smile, *dahlings!*"

"Trina!" Bryan whispers, and we both smile.

Trina snaps a photo, and another, then lunges forward, falling into us, and we all embrace, bouncing a little as we do.

"You're here!" she squeals.

"No, *you're* here!" I squeal back.

"You *guys!*" Bryan squeals.

A foursome of tourists in track jackets and walking shoes splits in half to walk around the little bouncing scrum we've formed on the sidewalk. Two of them stop and stare at us.

"They think we're famous," Bryan says.

"Or crazy," I say.

"What's the difference?" Trina says. "Don't you read *TMZ*? Fame and *loco* go hand in hand." She yells to the tourists, "You want a picture?" One takes out a camera, then another does. Soon all four are pointing cameras at us.

"You two, here," Bryan says, squaring his shoulders and crossing his arms. "One of you on each side. Straight backs, one leg forward. *Work it.*"

"I've never had my picture taken by a stranger before," I say. "At least not before breakfast."

Trina nudges me in the ribs. It's a riff on a line that Paul says to Holly in *Breakfast at Tiffany's*. She answers with Holly's line: "'We'll spend the day doing things we've never done before!'"

Bryan smooths his hair and holds out his hands, palms up. He mimics Audrey Hepburn's voice. "'We'll take turns. First something you've never done, then me.'"

I finish the quote. "'Of course, I can't think of anything *I've* never done.'"

The cameras flash and we laugh. Soon the tourists are joined by another photographer. "Are you famous?" he calls to us.

"Of course we are!" Trina yells back. "Aren't you?"

We pose for another round before the crowd shuffles away.

"Have a nice day, *dahlings*!" Trina yells after them, waving.

"Here we are," I say.

"Yes," Trina says.

"All of us," Bryan says.

"All of us," Trina and I repeat.

he first thing Bryan and Trina can think of that they've never done before is have breakfast in a New York City diner.

"Good thing that's the next item on our itinerary," I say. I reach into my hand-bag and pull out a printed copy of the day's schedule. "Says so right here."

"Oh, my God, you printed it out," Trina says.

"Phone batteries die," I say. "And I don't want to miss anything. We're only here for—"

"Don't finish that sentence," Bryan says. "I don't even want to think about going home."

"Me, either," Trina says. "As far as we're concerned, we're staying here forever. Our lives will be full of fancy parties and cocktails, just like Holly's!"

I smile. "Fine," I say. "But we still have a schedule."

"You're amazing," Trina says.

"I'm starving," Bryan says.

I pull out my iPhone. "I found one on Yelp that's right over on Third Avenue," I say. "The reviews say it's pretty good."

"How far is that?" Bryan says.

"A few blocks. We can walk it," I say.

"Ex-*squeeze* me?" Bryan says. "Walk? Have we met?"

"What, you don't walk?" Trina says.

Bryan backs up two steps and points to a big black SUV idling at the corner. A guy with a visored cap sits in the driver's seat. "Mademoiselles, your chariot awaits."

"You rented a car?" Trina says, framing it in her iPhone camera. "With a *driver*?"

Bryan shrugs. "I guess it comes with my room at the Four Seasons. My suite, I mean. They seemed to take pity on me when I told them how *gruesome* my flight was. I only exaggerated a little."

"How little?" I ask.

"Let's put it this way. I'm in the Imperial Suite now."

"The who?"

"It's more expensive than the Presidential."

A man in a gray cap opens the door to the backseat, driver's side.

"Of course it is," Trina says. "Hello," she says to the driver. "Can I take your picture?"

"Third Avenue, was it?" Bryan asks after we all slide in. The SUV pulls away from the curb.

I realize that riding in the back of a chauffeur-driven SUV is the most glamorous thing I've ever done in my life. "This qualifies," I say.

"As what?"

"Something I've never done before."

"Speaking of which," Trina says, looking at Bryan, "I can't believe you've never been to a diner before. I thought you came to New York all the time!"

Bryan shakes his head. "Yeah, but I always come with my parents, and they always want to eat at the same places. Eleven Madison Park. Jean-Georges. Per Se. You know. Places like that."

Trina blinks. "Huh? Eleven what? Jean who? Per what?"

"I think he means he's rich," I say. "The Akitos live large when they travel. First class. VIP. Four stars all the way."

"Five," Bryan says.

"Do your parents know you're here?" Trina asks Bryan.

"Are you kidding?" he says. "They'd never let me come alone. They wouldn't stop me from coming; they'd just insist on coming, too."

"Mine don't, either," Trina says. "My mom is going to kill me when she finds out."

"Mothers are like that," Bryan says. "What about yours, Gemma?"

I freeze for a split second. Things are going way too well to start talking about mothers. I don't want to go there. Not yet. I swallow and smile and weigh, for that split second, whether I should lie or not.

But I don't have to decide. Trina's too busy talking. "Fanciest place I ever go is Del Taco," she says. I wonder if she knows she just saved me.

"What's that?" I ask.

"Don't they have Del Taco on the East Coast?" she asks.

"I don't think so," I say. "At least, I've never heard of it."

"Thank God," she says. "All the more reason to stay here indefinitely." She smiles and changes the subject, gingerly patting her updo. "*Dahling*, how's my hair? Is it holding up? You have no idea how much Aqua Net I have up there."

"Oh, I think I do," I say, reaching over to tuck a stray strand behind her ear.

e slide into a vinyl booth near the back of the Empire State Royal Diner ahead of schedule, behind tables of businesspeople in pinstripes and groups of sunglasses-wearing slackers in torn T-shirts. We order coffees and pancakes, plus a plate of hash browns to share. "Extra crispy," Trina says to the waitress, who smiles and says, "Of course."

I stir two packets of sugar into my coffee, and then a third.

"A little coffee with your sugar?" Trina smiles.

"I know, I can't help it," I say as I drain the pitcher of half-and-half. The waitress replaces it immediately as she whisks by. "I love the smell, but I have to doctor it up to drink it."

Bryan looks over at my cup. "That's not a coffee. That's a milk shake." He winks. "Maybe that's what makes you so sweet." I fan myself in mock modesty.

"Oh, brother," Trina says. I kick her under the table and she puts her head on my shoulder.

Bryan takes a small pad of paper and a green pencil from his jacket pocket. He starts swiping the pencil across the paper.

"What are you drawing?" Trina asks him.

"A cocktail dress. Something I've had in my head all morning. Remember the dress that Holly Golightly wears when her husband, Doc, first comes to her apartment?"

"Oh, totally," I say. "The black one. With the feathers around the hem. Cocktail length."

"That's the one," he says, pencil scratching the paper.

"You don't sketch on an iPad or something?" Trina asks.

"Oh, no. The great ones never had iPads," Bryan says. "Can you see Edith Head sketching out Bette Davis's Bumpy Night dress from *All About Eve* on an iPad? No, no, I can't draw on those things. This isn't *Project Runway*. I'm old-school. I only sketch on paper. And while we're at it, I only read real books. I only wear leather shoes. I wear a watch that needs winding."

He pulls up his cuff to show us his Rolex. "Old-school," he says.

"Sorry," Trina says and rolls her eyes.

Bryan picks up his coffee cup with two hands. "Why were you so late, Trina?"

"Ask my pilot, *dahling*. The red-eye was, like, three hours delayed."

"Three hours?"

"And only two of those hours were because it was raining in Denver," Trina says. "It was too *gruesome*." Both Bryan and I laugh. It's a word Holly Golightly used: *gruesome*.

"Why on earth did you take a red-eye?" Bryan says.

"Because it's sixty dollars cheaper. That's, like, a shift and a half at the Copper Corral."

"Corral?"

"The restaurant I work at."

"It's called the Corral? Like, a corral where you put cows and pigs? Where you line them up at troughs and feed them corn and slop?"

"That's the idea," Trina says. "We fatten up our customers for market. You'd love it there."

Bryan throws his pencil at her, like they've known each other for years.

"Oh, my God," I say. "My hair hurts." I tug the tiara out of my hair and start feeling around for bobby pins.

"What are you doing?" Bryan says.

"I'm sorry. I can't take the updo another minute."

"Oh, Gemma. Dear Gemma. Glamour isn't painless, you know," Bryan says.

"*You* want to try this hairstyle?" Trina says.

Bryan sighs. "If you must, though I'd suggest you cover your shoulders with your wrap. Don't want those flakes of dried hairspray to gunk up the Givenchy. Or is it *faux-venchy?*"

"You'll never know," I say, batting my eyelashes.

"You're so perfect, Gemma."

"When are you two just going to make out?" Trina looks over at a customer at the next table and points at herself. "Third wheel."

"Very funny," I say. Obviously he was joking. My dress is anything but Givenchy, and I'm anything but perfect.

Our pancakes come. Trina takes a picture. "Instagram, *dahlings*," she says, tapping at her phone.

I drown my short stack in great glugs of maple syrup. Trina runs just a few squiggles of syrup across the top of her stack. Bryan carefully pours a small puddle onto the side of his plate. "I like to dunk my bites individually," he says.

"Is he for real?" Trina asks.

"Yep, I think so."

"Thank heavens, *dahling*!"

We devour our pancakes, smiling our way through bite after bite like little kids, totally ignoring the hash browns.

Finally, Trina drops her fork on her empty plate. "I'm never eating again."

I drain the last of my coffee.

"Subject change," Bryan says.

"Uh-oh," I say.

"Not you." He turns to Trina. "What's going on with . . . what's his name again?"

"Who?"

"You know who."

"Miles?"

"That's right. Miles."

Trina shakes her head. "Nothing."

"Nothing?"

"Nothing."

"It's OK if you don't want to talk about it," I say.

"Look, he dumped me, OK? Actually, he didn't even bother with that. He just changed his Facebook status to 'single.'"

"Are you kidding?" Bryan says. "What a wuss."

I take Trina's forearm. *"Quel beast,"* I say, quoting Holly Golightly again.

"Yeah, well, whatever," she says. "I should have known he was a freak. He took me to a mixed martial arts competition on our first date. Mixed martial arts! Who does that?"

"Charming," Bryan says. "And for your second date? Did he invite you over to watch monster trucks?"

"That would be funny if it weren't so close to the truth," Trina says. "But payback's coming for poor Miles."

"What do you mean?" I ask.

"I have pictures of him on my phone."

"So what?" I say.

"What *kind* of pictures?" Bryan asks, his eyes lighting up.

"Trust me, not the kind I wanted," Trina says. "He sent them to me."

"*That* kind?" Bryan says. "Let's see!"

"OK, but you won't be impressed," Trina says, swiping her finger across her smartphone.

"You guys! No junk at the table. Please."

Bryan winks at Trina. "Later."

"Where are you staying?" I ask Trina.

"I don't know yet," Trina says.

"What? Where did you get dressed? You look divine."

"Stop, *dahling*. I got dressed on the plane."

"Like, in the bathroom?" Bryan asks.

"You should have seen the look on the guy sitting next to me when I came back to my seat in this getup. I left wearing yoga pants, came back in a gown."

"And you did your hair in there, too? While the plane was still in the air?"

"You know it."

"That's the most fabulous thing I've ever heard," Bryan says.

"Fabulous is my middle name, *dahling*."

"You are a magician," Bryan says. *"Purrr..."*

"OK, your turn to make out now," I say. I look up at the passing waitress and point to myself. "Third wheel." She drops a new pitcher of half-and-half on the table.

"I'd say this is going well," Bryan says.

"What?" Trina says.

Bryan points at himself, then me, then Trina. "This. Us."

"I agree," I say.

"Ditto," Trina says. Almost without thinking, I hold my hands out, and Bryan and Trina each take one. Just for a second.

"Anyway, I'm glad you like it," Trina says. "My outfit, I mean. Because pretty much all you're going to see me in is this or the yoga pants I was wearing on the plane. The airline lost my checked suitcase. You know, the one with all five costume changes I was planning."

"No," I say.

"Yes," she says.

"So, what you're saying is, you're wearing this same outfit to the Ziegfeld tonight?" Bryan is aghast.

"I know. *Quelle horreur!*" Trina says. "But what else can I do?" She strung out the word *do*, making an O with her mouth and widening her eyes, fake-surprised, Audrey-style.

Bryan looks back and forth at us across the table. "OK, that settles it. After breakfast, we're going shopping."

"Shopping?" I say. "That's not on the itinerary. I don't know if we'll have—"

"It's an emergency," Bryan says. "And you're both staying with me in my suite at the Four Seasons."

"But," I say, "I'm already in a room at the Malcolm."

"And I'm broke," Trina says. "I spent every penny I had on my plane ticket."

"Has either one of you ever stayed at the Four Seasons before? In the Imperial Suite?"

"Duh," Trina says. "No."

"Then it fits in perfectly with today's theme. Now pipe down. I'm taking you shopping. And the Four Seasons will be happy to send over to the Malcolm for your luggage. I'll just call them."

"You don't need to—"

"End of discussion," he says. "Adjust the itinerary if you would, Ms. Social Director. If you two are going to be my arm candy tonight, you're going to need to be smashing. Like, Givenchy smashing."

"Bryan—"

"And, Gemma, *ne worry pas*. There are two bedrooms in

the suite. If what's his name shows up, Trina can sleep with me."

"What's-his-name?"

"Dusty," he says, smiling and leaning forward. "Remember him?"

"Yeah, right," I say. I kick Bryan under the table. "As if."

"Dusty," Trina says. "What's the latest?"

"What do you mean?" I blush. I try not to, but I blush.

"Oh, give it a rest, Gemma. We know there's something going on there."

I look up to see the waitress standing at our booth. "Coffee?"

She pours before I can answer.

"I don't get crushes on boys I've never met," I say, stirring a packet of sugar into my cup.

gasp when we walk into Bryan's suite at the Four Seasons. I put my hand against the wall to hold myself up. I've never seen anything like it, even in a movie. It's huge. Five rooms. Wait, no—six rooms. Panoramic views of the city. A wraparound terrace overlooking Central Park, with trees. Trees on the terrace! Two bedrooms with huge beds piled with pillows, three and four rows deep. Three massive marble-and-glass bathrooms with floor-to-ceiling windows looking out at the city. ("Can people see in?" I ask. "Who cares?" Trina says. "When you're this rich, screw it!") Walk-in closets bigger than our whole apartment back in Philadelphia. A huge kitchen with an eight-burner stove—you know, for warming up the coffee that comes from room service. And a separate dining area to sit and nibble on strawberries and sip champagne while you contemplate your day.

And a grand piano.

A *grand piano*! It shines, glossy and black, in the bay windows overlooking the city. I sit down on the bench, hiking up my skirt daintily. I sway one hand through the air. I'm Liberace. I sweep the other hand across the keys, lowest to highest and back again.

"I'm totally getting this on Instagram," Trina says, framing me in her iPhone. "*And* Vine."

"Do you play?" Bryan asks.

"The piano? Uh, no," I answer, taking my hands off the keys.

"I can have someone sent up if you'd like a serenade. I'm sure they have at least one professional piano player on staff."

"No, thanks," Trina says. "Piano seren*ahh*des are so déclassé. I mean, they're all right for older women, but . . ." It's another phrase from *Breakfast*.

"If they could send up a string quartet, however, I might consider it," Trina says. "*Dahling.*"

"You're such a princess," Bryan says. He picks up the phone on the desk. "Front desk? We'll need a car, please, in about an hour. A big one. We're shopping. An Escalade? Perfect."

I go from room to room in the suite, sitting in every chair. There are easy chairs big enough to drown in, situated in front of plasma televisions. Desk and table chairs in shiny mahogany with brocaded fabric on the seats. And beds! A huge king bed in one room, and a pair of queens in another. I take a running leap onto one of the queens but can barely reach the middle. Trina immediately piles on top of me.

"This is insane!" she says. "It's marvelous! Simply marvelous!"

"Who stays in rooms like this?" I ask, wriggling out from underneath her.

"Actually, you'd be surprised at the kinds of people who stay here. You'd think it's all movie stars and supermodels, but really it's mostly people no one's ever heard of," Bryan says, drawing back the bedroom curtain. "Ladies, your view."

We both sit up on our knees. I gasp. Central Park, brilliant green in the morning sun, stretches into the distance northward, studded with sparkling lakes and ringed by beautiful limestone apartment towers. The sky, now periwinkle blue, has no clouds and is never-ending above us.

"Wow," I manage.

"Just how rich are you?" Trina asks.

Bryan shakes his head. "No comment."

I reach up, grab Bryan, and pull him down onto the bed with us.

"Can you adopt me?" I say.

"OK, girls," he says. "Let's get serious. We have less than sixteen hours until we need to be at the Ziegfeld. Actually, less than fifteen. I have every intention of being there at least an hour early, to ogle the crowd."

"The crowd?" Trina says.

"The crowd," Bryan says. "You don't think this screening is going to be attended by a bunch of schlubs, do you?"

"It's true," I say. "Every Audrey Hepburn fanatic on the planet will be there."

"The competition is going to be ferocious. And you'll be going in the nude if we don't get to Barneys and start dropping some cash," Bryan says.

"But—"

"But nothing. Dresses are on me."

"I don't need anything," I say, digging through my suit-case. "I have an outfit already prepared."

"Let's see!" Trina says.

"Not a chance," I say. "It's a surprise. But I'll come along. Just let me rinse off and change. I can't go shopping in an evening gown." I pull out a white and black picnic dress and a camel cardigan.

"Cute," Bryan says.

"Secondhand," I say. I wink at Trina.

I step into the bathroom with the outfit slung over my forearm and my makeup bag in my teeth.

"I won't be a minute," I say. I close the door. I can't believe how beautiful it is in here. Marble everywhere, and mirrors from floor to ceiling. The shower is the size of a walk-in closet, with the showerhead right in the middle of the ceiling, five feet above my head and dripping water like a tropical waterfall, warm and soft. I want to stand in it for an hour. But we have things to do.

I towel off, slip into my dress, clasp my hair into a ponytail, and slide on a pair of ballet slippers. I'm ready.

Back in the living room, Trina is buttoning her shirt, a pale blue men's oxford. "How's my hair?" she asks.

I hand her a scarf. "Here." She ties it around her hair. Perfect. She smooths the tails of her shirt over her yoga pants.

"Oh, dear," Bryan says.

"What?" Trina says.

"You weren't kidding about the yoga pants." He wraps a black cotton scarf around his neck, adjusting the drape over one shoulder. "We really are in a crisis."

*T*his way, ladies," Bryan says as we exit the elevator. "Next stop, Barneys. They carry Givenchy there."

The lobby of the Four Seasons is busy with people coming and going—checking in, checking out, waiting for cabs, asking the concierge whether they can get a last-minute lunch reservation at Le Bernardin (*A corner table, please*) or find someone to walk Poopska the Pekinese. There seem to be only two kinds of people here: really rich people and the people who work for them. Sometimes it's not easy to tell the difference.

"What about vintage?" I ask. "Maybe we should go to a consignment shop, one of the fancy ones. We could find an old Givenchy there. I mean, wouldn't an original Givenchy, one that could have been made by Givenchy himself, be better than a current one that he had nothing to do with?"

"No way," Bryan says. "Think about it. Audrey never wore old clothes, except in movies sometimes. She always dressed *au courant*. Do you think she'd be wearing a 1960s outfit if she were alive today?"

"He makes a point," Trina says. "She really was ahead of her time, not behind."

"I do," Bryan agrees. "I mean, her dresses look vintage to us now, but they were modern at the time. Besides, haven't we had enough of a retro moment? You know, standing outside Tiffany's in period costume? At six in the morning? Which, may I add, corresponds to three A.M. in Bel-Air."

"Yes," I say, but I'm not so sure. I always prefer vintage clothes. And I can't imagine Audrey in Versace.

We make our way through the crowded lobby and toward the front door. "Pardon us," Bryan says to a threesome of gray-haired women in bouclé jackets and big globe sunglasses walking arm in arm through the lobby. He thrusts out his arm to hold us back while the women pass. They're laughing together, like ancient friends.

"That's us one day," Trina says.

"I'm the one in the middle," Bryan says. "With the leopard-print scarf."

We flank Bryan, tucking our arms into his elbows, and step in unison toward the exit.

"To Barneys!" Bryan says.

Just before we reach the door, a figure steps in front of us. A small, roundish girl, wearing a black T-shirt that doesn't quite cover her stomach, which is spilling out over a pair of black jeans. She's short, maybe five feet. A camouflage hat covers her eyes, and a purple JanSport pack hangs off one shoulder. I almost trip over her foot.

"Gemma?" says the girl, reaching out to catch my fall.

The three of us stop. I cock my head backward and tighten my grip on Bryan. "I'm sorry?"

"Bryan?" the girl says, pointing at Bryan.

Bryan takes a slow step backward. "You must be mistaken."

"I'm not mistaken," says the girl. She thrusts her hand into her backpack and pulls out a piece of paper, a photograph of Bryan in a pair of postman shorts and a blazer at his junior class picnic, printed from his Facebook page. "It's you."

Trina takes a step forward. "What's this about?"

"And you," she says, fumbling in her knapsack. "You must be Trina." She holds up a photo of Trina, a selfie she took in her uniform from the Copper Corral.

Trina turns to me and scrunches her eyebrows. "Is this on the itinerary?"

I don't answer.

"Do I call for security, or do you?" Bryan asks. He clears his throat, ready to shout.

"No! Wait, don't," says the girl. She holds up her hand. "Can I talk to you guys for a minute?"

"My mother told me never to talk to strangers," Trina says.

"I'm not a stranger."

"Who are you and what do you want?" Bryan asks.

"I'm sorry to surprise you like this," says the girl. She takes off her camouflage hat and looks at the floor. "I'm Telly."

"What?" Trina says. "Could you repeat that?"

"Telly. My name is Telly. From your Tumblr page? *Oh Yeah, Audrey!*?"

"Oh, my God," I say. "It's you."

'm sorry for all the stuff I posted on the Tumblr page," Telly says after we have all filed out of the Four Seasons and onto the Fifty-seventh Street sidewalk. "I'm really not that, you know, mean. I just, I don't know why, but sometimes I get—"

An ambulance whizzes by, siren blaring, drowning Telly out before she can finish her thought. The sidewalk is full of tourists and ladies who look like they're heading for the salon. A pair of girls in high pigtails saunter past. A pair of young guys in jeans with snaps on the pockets follow them.

"Sometimes you get what?" I ask, stern.

She hooks her thumbs into her JanSport straps and looks across the street. Ice-blue eyes, pale skin. I can tell she's a beautiful girl, a bit younger than we are, but she seems exhausted.

"You just get what?" Trina barks. "Stupid?"

"Stupid? Or jealous?" Bryan says and looks down at Telly's muffin-top. "I can't imagine why." He raises his eyebrow in a harsh, snarky way, and it makes me feel bad for Telly.

"I said I'm sorry," Telly says. "I'm trying to make up for it."

"For what?" Trina says. "For being a moron? Good luck with that." She steps toward Telly, straightening her back to make herself look even taller than she is.

"I don't do it on purpose," Telly says. "I don't know if you'd understand. But it's, like, when I see really skinny girls like Audrey Hepburn or whoever I just get—"

I really want this moment to end. I want the three of us to get back to our perfect day, itinerary or not. It's all been going so well. And I don't like seeing this side of Bryan and Trina. It feels almost cruel.

"Look," I say, hoping to speed this moment up and get out of here. "We accept your apology, Telly, we really do. But we have things to do and not a lot of time. No offense."

"Wait a minute, Gemma," Bryan says, slowly removing his tortoiseshell sunglasses. "Not so fast. *I'm* offended." He turns toward Telly and waves his sunglasses in her face. "What did you just say? 'Skinny girls like Audrey Hepburn or whoever'? What do you mean, 'whoever'? This is Audrey Hepburn you're talking about!"

"It's OK, Bryan," I say, surprised that he wants to get into this. "Why don't we just go?" I take his forearm.

"Well?" Bryan asks.

Telly looks up at Bryan. "Listen. I didn't get it at first, but now I do. When I first came to your Tumblr page all I saw was another super-skinny girl in fancy clothes and it annoyed me. But then I started wondering why the three of you were so obsessed with her and I eventually looked her up."

"And?" Trina says.

"And I learned about her. And I rented some of her movies. And I read her biography."

"And?" Trina says again.

"And now I understand," Telly says.

"Understand what?" Bryan says.

"That she was amazing. *Is* amazing. I mean, all that work she did for UNICEF. Did you see the *Life* magazine photos of her in Ethiopia during that famine in the 1980s? Holding those starving children like they were her own?" Suddenly Telly is talking fast. "I did a paper on her for my world history class last week. I know, you aren't usually supposed to write about movie stars for history class, but I've never been a big fan of history class anyway, so I convinced my teacher to let me write about celebrities and humanitarian work and how when famous people get involved with a cause, it influences other people to get involved, too. More money gets raised and more people get help. Audrey Hepburn is the perfect example of that. I mean, I know I used to hate her for being so pretty and everything, but when I looked at what she did, I became a fan. I got an A on my paper, which was the first A that I ever got in history. Anyway, she was one of the first famous people to acknowledge tragedies. And to get so close to them. I mean, way before Angelina Jolie. Audrey really cared about other people more than herself. Who cares about her clothes?"

"Who *cares* about her *clothes?*" Bryan asks with astonishment, getting angrier with each word. But Telly doesn't take a breath.

"I even read this one book when I was working on the paper and she was quoted as saying something about how her greatest ambition wasn't to be a movie star, it was to be a mother. I mean, isn't that the total opposite of pretty much every other celebrity in the universe? All anyone ever thinks about these days is how to be the next reality star or whatever, and they're all just so fake, and not that I'm, like, dying to be a mother anytime soon, but I *would* like to be able to make a difference in someone else's life. Maybe it'll be a kid of my own or maybe it'll be another kid who needs help. I don't know.

Studying Audrey Hepburn really opened my eyes to that kind of thing. To being there for other people."

As she's talking, I'm watching her eyes, and I can see that she means what she's saying. Maybe she talks a lot, but she talks like someone who has something important to say and needs to say it. Telly sounds like someone who is almost . . . I don't know . . . *wise*. Someone who's learned something about life and gets it. Like she sees beyond Audrey Hepburn's obvious beauty and straight into something *deeper*.

Telly takes a breath. "It's what matters most, you know," she says. She nods at me, as though she's saying it just for me to hear. "*Being there* when others choose to walk away."

"*Dahling!*" Trina yells, interrupting Telly. "You've made your point. You like Audrey Hepburn. Congratulations. We have to go." She turns to me. "Aren't we on some kind of schedule?"

"I guess we are," I say. I wrinkle my forehead as if to say to Telly, *I'm sorry.*

"Wait another minute," Bryan says, grabbing Trina's arm. "I want to know exactly how this girl found us in the first place."

Telly reaches back into her knapsack and pulls out her smartphone. "Instagram." She swipes her finger across the screen—first a picture Trina took of me playing the grand piano (#fourseasons), then the pancakes (#dinerbreakfast), then a photo of me and Bryan out on Fifth Avenue from this morning (#hollyandpaul), then a selfie under the Tiffany's sign (#diamonds).

"That's a cute one," Trina mutters, pointing at the selfie. "Still, it's kind of stalkery for you to have all these. It's disturbing." She scowls.

"I'm not stalking you," Telly says. I can tell she means it. "I'm really sorry."

"You said that already," Bryan says. "The question is, what exactly is your point? What do you want?" He looks her up and down again. "Fashion tips?"

"That's enough," I say as I see Telly wince. Bryan softens.

"I don't want anything. There's just something I thought you'd want to know about. Look at this." Telly holds out a newspaper, folded open to a small article next to a photograph of Audrey Hepburn. "Right here, at the top of the page."

Bryan swipes the paper from her and starts to read.

HEPBURN WARDROBE
TO BE AUCTIONED TODAY

Call her the eternal muse. The ultimate fashionista. And now, the saleswoman of the year.

Audrey Hepburn's personal wardrobe—45 pieces kept in cold storage by her estate since her death two decades ago—will be auctioned off at an exclusive sale today at noon.

The items on the block range from a simple pillbox hat valued at $4,000 to the iconic black gown worn by Hepburn in the opening credits of Breakfast at Tiffany's—*a gown Sotheby's expects to fetch north of $100,000.*

Many of the lots are one-of-a-kind pieces created by famed French couturier Hubert de Givenchy, the flamboyant designer who frequently called Hepburn his muse. Givenchy, now 86, lives in France.

All the profits from the auction will go to UNICEF, the United Nations charity that channels aid to impoverished children around the globe. It's an organization Hepburn was closely associated with. Sotheby's hopes to take in more than a million dollars by the end of the afternoon.

"On their own merits, the clothes would be beautiful," said Steven Kolb, Executive Director of the Council of Fashion Designers of America. "But what makes them so special is that they belonged to one of the most fashionable and beautiful women in history, Audrey Hepburn."

"We expect aggressive bidding," said a source close to the sale. "Audrey Hepburn has international appeal, and French design from the mid-century is hot right now, especially in Asia. I bet a lot of this stuff will end up in Japan and China."

"Wow," I say. "What I wouldn't give to see that. Can you imagine being in the same room with the hat she wears when she says 'How do I look?' to Paul on her way out the door to go see Sally Tomato in jail?"

"No kidding," Trina says, her face softening to a smile. "Or that trench coat she wears at the end, when she goes looking for Cat, the cat, in the alley in the rain?"

"Right?" Telly says. "Or that pink dress she's wearing when she finds out what happened to Fred? Remember? When she's starting to date the Brazilian, José da Silva Pereira, who of course dumps her after she gets arrested for taking the weather report from Sally Tomato . . ."

I look at Trina. "She clearly knows her stuff," I say.

"What's your point?" Trina says.

I take Trina's arm and Bryan's, and we form a little circle a few steps away from Telly. "Look, I'm just saying, I think we should go."

"But what about the itinerary?" Trina says.

"We can change it," I say. "Just a little. Just enough to go to the auction. I mean, it's spontaneous. Don't you think Audrey would have gone? I mean, Holly. What do you think, Bryan?"

"Of course we should go," Bryan says.

"She's not coming, is she?" Trina asks. She and Bryan look over at Telly, who is tapping on her smartphone. Her backpack starts to slip off her shoulder and she hoists it back on.

"I think we should ask her to come," I say. "I think she's nice. I mean, we wouldn't even know about the auction unless—"

Trina raises an eyebrow and looks over at Telly, then at Bryan, then back at me. "If she promises to use fewer words," she says, loudly enough for Telly to hear.

"Sorry," Telly says, stepping closer to us. "I just sometimes, I don't know, get kind of mixed up about what I want to say and how I want to say it and—"

"Stop!" Trina says. She holds her finger up. "That's what I'm talking about."

"I'll try," Telly says. She shrugs and smiles. It's an honest smile, like she's relieved.

Bryan is already on his phone. "Hello, Sotheby's?"

e tries for twenty minutes, but Bryan can't get on the Sotheby's guest list—even a platinum card has limits. But he convinces us we should try to go anyway. "Let's just show up. If we act like we belong there, maybe they'll let us in. And if not, we'll just pretend we're with someone else, someone who's already inside."

"Like who? How are we going to know who's inside?" Trina asks.

"It doesn't make any difference," he says. "You can get in

almost anywhere if you call yourself a 'personal assistant,' you know. Just pick a fancy name, like Dalton or de La Croix. 'I'm Ms. Dalton's assistant,' Try it."

"Are you sure?" I ask.

"I know it's not on the itinerary," Bryan says. "But, Gemma, have you ever crashed an auction before?"

"Um, no?"

"Trina?"

"No."

"And what's the theme for our day?"

Trina and I nod. "Right," she says.

"What's the theme?" Telly asks.

Trina and I just look at each other and smile.

"What's the theme?" Telly asks again. "Guys?"

"Should we tell her?" I say.

"Let her figure it out," Trina says. "It's a test." She smiles at Telly. It's a half smile, but it's something.

"We're at least going to try," Bryan says. "What's the worst that can happen? They kick us out and we go back to plan A: Barneys. Are you with me?"

"Yes, sir," Trina says with a mock salute.

"I'm in!" I say, thrusting my hand in the air.

"What's the theme?" Telly asks.

I am bewildered and astonished and *so* excited—just hours ago I was standing in a shared bathroom in a cheap hotel, and now I'm driving through the Upper East Side in a huge black SUV from the Four Seasons. Bryan asks the driver to take a roundabout route, pointing out some of the most expensive shops in the world as we drive past: Armani, Valentino, Chanel. Names I've only read in magazines but never knew I'd ever see.

"Maybe we should just stop at Barneys," Trina says. "You did say no vintage, and obviously everything at the auction is going to be vintage." She's joking, of course.

"Um, I think this qualifies as an exception, right, Bryan?" I say as we pass Barneys.

"Girls, focus, please. What we're going to see is way beyond 'vintage.' These are museum-quality pieces. And I don't want to get your hopes up, but I have a feeling the stuff will be too pricey even for me. I mean, even *I* have my limits."

"Bryan, you disappoint me," Trina says. "Where's that good old Bel-Air optimism?"

I smack Trina on the arm. "It'll be good inspiration," I say. "For when we go shopping later."

"I'm not going in," Telly says.

"What?" I say. "Why not?"

"Look at me!" Telly says. "I'm in jeans. I have a JanSport backpack on!"

"You? What about me, *dahlings*?" Trina asks. "I'm in yoga pants. Would Audrey Hepburn ever wear yoga pants to a public event?"

"If she did," I say, "she'd make them look fabulous. Just like you do."

Trina scowls. "No, seriously. Yoga pants!"

"She's right, Trina," Bryan says. "Yoga pants look rich, like you're rich enough not to care. Like you're just fitting in this auction between a visit to the nutritionist and a pedicure. Like pawing over a bunch of dresses worn by the most beautiful woman in history is a big yawn."

"Uh-huh," Trina says, obviously not believing him.

"But what about me?" Telly says. "I'm in jeans, and I feel like a slob and . . . forget it. I'll just wait out here. You guys go in."

"You're coming," I say. "We wouldn't even be here without you."

Bryan grabs Telly's cap. "Give me that." He stuffs it into her backpack. "Smooth down your hair. Who has a rubber band?"

I unclasp my still-wet ponytail and hand my clip to Bryan. He pulls Telly's hair into a low chignon and secures it. "There." He unwraps the scarf from his neck and hands it to her. "Don't wrap it, just drape it down the front so it covers your T-shirt." He holds up his sunglasses. "And put these on."

Telly is transformed.

"Yes," Bryan says. "You almost look the part. Close enough anyway. You could be an artist or something. It's a good thing you wore all black."

The SUV pulls up to the curb in front of a shiny glass and steel building. "Sotheby's," says the driver.

"Thank you, sir," Telly says. She hands him a one-dollar bill. "A tip."

Bryan ducks behind Telly and slips the driver a twenty, winking at me as he does it.

A pair of women push through the glass doors, one carrying a shiny leather Birkin bag (I'd recognize it anywhere), the other, an even larger bag of pale brown leather with several pockets, each capped with a gold clasp. They have matching chignons, and one is wearing a nearly blinding diamond cuff on one wrist.

"I don't know about this," Telly says, hiking her backpack up onto her shoulders.

"The backpack stays in the SUV," Bryan says, tossing it into the car. "Now, remember, girls. We *belong* here."

Trina whispers into my ear, "Yeah, right."

"I heard that," Bryan says. "Listen. Here's the magic trick. If you act like you belong here, no one will question you. No one will care what you're wearing. If you want to be important, act important. Got it? Now march."

He leads the way through the glass doors and into Sotheby's.

t the top of the stairs, a man in a black suit hands me a catalog: *Audrey's Closet: An Exclusive Event for Elite Collectors of Iconic Couture.* I open to a random page and read aloud. "'Lot 3. Black duchess cocktail dress, 1958.' What's a 'lot'?"

"It's what they call the items for sale. Lots," Bryan says, his neck craning to take in the room, which is slowly filling with women in extremely expensive-looking shoes.

"Oh," I say, slightly ashamed that I didn't know that.

"Lot 3 is valued at fifteen thousand dollars." I gasp. Fifteen thousand dollars!

"What else is in there?" Trina asks.

I read on. "'Lot 11. Crocodile handbag, 1961, valued at seven thousand dollars.'" I flip a page. "'Lot 16. Faconne satin evening jacket with lace overlay, 1965, valued at twenty-two thousand dollars.' Oh, my God."

"What's your point?" Bryan says, still looking around. "I've never seen so much Chanel in one room."

"Twenty-two thousand dollars is my point," I say, finding the picture of the jacket in the brochure. I know I shouldn't be so impressed by the prices, but I can't help it. I can't imagine a dress costing twenty-two thousand dollars.

"That's like a car," Telly says.

"You guys are so cute," Bryan says. "Put that catalog away. Look around! Let's go see the real thing. We still have a half hour to look at the lots up close before the bidding starts. And Trina," he says, grabbing her by the hips, "stand up straight. Try to look like you belong here. If you're going to pass for rich in those yoga pants, you're going to have to work a little harder."

Trina punches him on the arm, and we walk past the auction room to the display room.

It's a wonderland.

A dozen platforms, each about three feet high and six feet square, dot the room. Atop each one stand four mannequins, each in a different outfit. Most of them wear black—dresses, suits, evening gowns. A few wear white. A pale gray cowl-neck sweater hangs over one. I recognize so many of them. "Look!" I say, grabbing Trina's arm. "There's the sweater she wore at the police station!"

"Yes!" she squeaks. "And over there! It's the dress she changes into for the party in her apartment!"

Bryan is just silent. He's staring intently at the room. I don't know if he's overwhelmed or what. "Are you OK?" I ask.

"Oh, yeah," he says. "Game face."

Women in brightly colored suits and artificially colored hair stroll around the room in groups of two and three, pointing to the clothes and pointing out details to one another. Two men, one in a wheelchair, circle the perimeter, carefully taking notes on an iPad. A young man and woman lean on one of the platforms, talking in Chinese. A guard taps one of them on the shoulder and motions for them to stand up. He points at a discreet sign on one wall: PLEASE DO NOT LEAN ON THE PLATFORMS. Waiters walk among the crowd with trays of glasses filled with champagne and stacks of little triangle-shaped sandwiches.

"*Boudoir* sandwiches!" Bryan says. "How *chic*."

"*What* sandwiches?" Telly asks.

"Boudoir. The kind of thing you nibble on while you powder your nose. Have one," Bryan says, waving down a waiter.

"Cucumber or pâté?" the waiter asks.

I take in a breath, a deep one. I hold it a moment, eyes
closed. I'm anxious and excited and terrified and thrilled,
all at the same time. And I have that feeling that something's
going to happen, something big and exhilarating and danger-
ous, like when you're on a roller coaster and you've ratcheted
your way to the top of the first hill. *Click, click, click.* And then
the clicks start to slow down, and you feel the front of the car
start to drop. You want to scream, but you hold it in. Then you
feel yourself dropping, slowly at first, then faster, and you
know that full speed, straight down, is just in front of you, so
tantalizingly close . . .

Up until now, it's been just us. Our own little crew, talking
about the weekend, about one another, about Audrey, like
we knew her better than anyone else possibly could. Like
she belongs to us, and only us, because no one could love her
more.

But now here we are, surrounded by Audrey Hepburn.
By her clothes, by her aura, by her *people*. There are probably
people here who even knew her. And people who would—and
could—spend thousands of dollars just to own something she
wore, just to be that much closer to her. So much closer to her
than I'll ever be.

Oh, I wish I could wear every one of these dresses. I never knew I had that dream until now. But it feels like a dream I've had every night of my life.

I *should* feel like an impostor. But something tells me I *belong* here. Me, Gemma Beasley.

I feel my phone vibrate. It's a text from Dad. *Hi, honey. Are you up?*

I don't text back. He still thinks I'm at Casey's. And that we haven't even woken up yet. He has no clue.

ubbles!" exclaims Trina, waving at a waiter. "Over here, *dahling*!"

"Do you think we're allowed?" I whisper. I've only had champagne once before, and that was just a sip at midnight that Mom gave me on New Year's Eve once. I fell asleep about four minutes later. And we're not old enough to drink.

"Ever had champagne before noon before?" Trina asks.

I shake my head.

"Well, then."

"Don't mind if we do," Bryan says to the waiter, taking two glasses from the tray and handing one to Trina and one to me. He takes two more. "Where's Telly?"

"Right here," Telly says from behind him.

He hands her a glass of champagne.

Trina grabs my elbow. "Oh, my God," she says, dragging me to a brown-and-white-checked "traveling suit, 1959," on a nearby platform. "Look at that belt. It sits so high on her waist!"

"And look!" I say, pointing at one right behind Trina. "There's the one Bryan was sketching this morning!" I exclaim. A group of women turn to look at me. I'm obviously being too loud. I smile at them. "Sorry," I say. I raise my glass. "Cheers," I whisper, and sip my champagne.

I move closer to the black jersey dress with the feathers at the hem, Lot 14. "You only see it for a few seconds in the movie." I reach out to run my hand along the waist. "Oh, I love this dress. Look at the drawstring!" I flick the tiny bow. The sign says: VALUED AT $4,000.

"Pardon me, miss," says a waiter, wagging a finger at me. He points at a sign at the mannequin's feet: PLEASE DO NOT TOUCH THE GARMENTS, it says.

"Oops," I say, snapping my hand back and almost knocking Telly's champagne out of her hand. "I'm sorry." I giggle. Am I tipsy? I take another sip.

"It's the dress Holly is wearing when Doc comes to her apartment to try and convince her to move back to Texas," I say to Telly.

"I totally remember," Telly says. "She's late for dinner at the '21' Club, and Paul knocks on her door and calls her Lulamae, and she thinks it's because her brother Fred is there, but it's not Fred, it's Doc, and then—"

"Look at the skirt, that flippy layer of fringe. The shape is so classic, but that flirty little attachment at the bottom of the skirt—remember how it moves when she jumps up in Doc's arms?" I swish my hands back and forth at my knees.

"And the attached rhinestone brooch," Telly says. "The whole thing is—"

"Four thousand dollars!" I squeal.

The women turn and look at me again. I smile at them. "Sorry," I whisper. I put a hand to my mouth.

"I don't know. It's just so weird, don't you think?" Trina says. *"Dahling?"*

"What's weird about it?" I say. I sip.

"I don't mean the dress is weird," Trina says. "I mean, the way Holly acts like she's still in love with Doc or something. The way she acts so excited to see him when he shows up, even though she ran away from him. She left him in Texas, you know? She took off and changed her name! She didn't ever want to see him again!"

"Yeah, but," Bryan says, "Holly still kind of loved Doc. Don't you see? Even though she left him. She didn't leave him because she hated him. She left him—left everything—because she wanted to be someone else. She knew she didn't belong in Tulip, Texas. Think about it. She was always acting like a lost little girl in that movie. Living in that apartment with hardly any furniture. Sitting out on the fire escape and sneaking up to the apartment above to see Paul Varjak. Pretending not to know what Sally Tomato was really up to even though she was going to jail to visit him. All she wanted was for people to like her. Anyone—gangsters, ex-husbands—whoever. She just didn't want to get too close to anyone. She just wanted, you know, affection."

For a second, lost in his words, it almost feels like he's talking about me. I wanted people to like me, too. I wanted affection. But sometimes it's easier to get people to like you if you don't let them get too close. As soon as you open up, they start to find reasons to not like you. Or to feel sorry for you.

"Is that what they call it, Dr. Freud?" Trina says. "*Affection?*" She shakes her head and takes another sip of champagne. "I don't know. Sometimes it seems more like a transaction when she's getting fifty dollars for the powder room!"

"That's not how I see it," I say. "I mean, what is she supposed to do? She's in the city by herself, you know? She has to make a living somehow. And once you start getting fifty dollars to go to the powder room, it's not easy to give it up for a job checking coats at a dollar fifty an hour."

"Good point," Trina says. "If anyone gave me fifty dollars to hit the ladies' room you can bet I'd ditch my job at the Corral. Pronto."

This is dangerously close to a game of speculation about what Holly Golightly did or didn't do for a living in the movie— or worse, a fight about it. I don't know how many times I've deleted comments from *Oh Yeah, Audrey!* about how Holly Golightly was really just a prostitute. She might have hung out with rich men and accepted their money and gifts, but she definitely didn't sleep with them. Definitely. I don't even like to think about it.

Bryan seems to sense my annoyance, and he breaks the silence with a subject change: back to fashion. "Do you remember the hat she was wearing in that scene?" He makes a motion over his head, tracing the shape of a tall, flat-topped hat. "It was like something between a fez and a pillbox, very London bobby with the fur appliqué on the front."

"Yes, white fur!" Trina says.

"Like a little snowball of fur!" Telly says, motioning to show where it was on the hat, smack-dab in the middle.

"And feathers! Little black feathers sticking out! Remember? Feathers!" I say, or maybe I yell it, because a bunch of people turn to look at me again.

"I'm sorry," I say, shrugging to no one in particular and turning back to the dress. "Could you imagine wearing such a beautiful dress?" I can't wait to see it on that massive Ziegfeld screen tonight.

"You would look great in it, Gemma," Trina says. "It would be such a good length for you."

"Yeah, right, Trina! Like I'd even fit into it," I say, though even as I say it, my mind is racing, picturing myself in the dress, the four-thousand-dollar dress, spinning in front of a mirror, then out for a fancy dinner somewhere, with Paul, a.k.a. Fred, and maybe to a cocktail party or dancing or just walking the streets of the city, holding hands and staying out all night, not coming home until morning, being someone else, being Holly, being Audrey, in this beautiful dress . . . "Be serious," I say.

"A girl can always dream," Trina says. "Right, Bryan?"

"Always," Bryan says. He kisses me on the cheek. "Always."

*L*adies and gentlemen, the auction will begin in five minutes in the main auction room. Please take your seats."

I follow the others into the auction room, which is filled with cushioned fold-up chairs and people wearing dark suits and holding white paddles with numbers on them. They're milling around, looking for seats. Some clearly want to be up front; others crowd toward the back.

I wobble a little as I snake my way to a seat near the back.

It's only just getting on noon and I have had a glass and a half of champagne. Which is about a glass more than I've ever had in my life.

Trina hands me a triangle sandwich and sits down next to me. "Isn't this lovely?" she asks. "*Dahling?*"

"Divine," I say, scarfing down the sandwich so fast I don't even know what's in it.

"How dainty," Bryan says, handing me his sandwich, too.

"Chicken salad?" I ask.

"Chopped liver," he says.

"I hate chopped liver," I say, swallowing and holding my hand out for another one.

Trina cracks up. "You're awesome," she says.

"No, I'm starving," I correct her.

"Shh!" Bryan says. "It's starting."

he auctioneer stands at the front of the room, behind a lectern on a small platform. A mannequin is wheeled in, wearing what looks like a raincoat. The 150 people or so in the audience lean into one another, whispering. The lots are rolled out, one after another, and displayed.

"Lot 13. Khaki trench coat, impermeable treated cotton, 1960. One of the few items offered today not created by Monsieur de Givenchy. This simple but impeccable overcoat was designed by Paco Rabanne and worn by Miss Hepburn in several photographs made in the early months of 1961. It is valued at three thousand dollars."

The first paddle shoots up almost immediately. "Three," says a young, well-groomed black man sitting next to an elegant Asian woman with jet-black hair pulled tight into a chignon.

"Who is that woman?" I say. "She's beautiful."

"That's Yoko Shimada," Bryan says. "And her agent, I guess."

"Who?" Trina says.

"She's a Japanese actress," he says. "She's super famous back in Japan. My mother loves her."

"Does she live in New York now?" I ask.

"I doubt it. I bet she came from Tokyo just for this auction. They are obsessed with Audrey Hepburn in Japan. *Obsessed*."

"They can't be as obsessed as we are," I say.

"You have no idea," Bryan says.

"Three thousand five," says a gray-haired woman in a brocade jacket sitting just behind the slick-haired man, as she flashes her paddle. She rolls the r in *three*, which makes her sound like she's from far away. Maybe Argentina or someplace exotic.

The man puts his paddle under his arm and shakes his head.

"Three thousand five hundred is our current bid. Any others?" No paddles go up.

"Last chance?"

No one bids.

"Done. Next item, please," the auctioneer says.

"I'll be right back," Telly says, stepping over a couple toward the aisle.

fter several lots—including a red
gown Audrey Hepburn wore in
Funny Face and a simple shift from
Sabrina, a young woman in a black
shirt wheels out another mannequin. It's the one wearing the
dress I'd just been gushing over in
the other room. I gasp.

"Lot 14," the auctioneer says. "Black jersey day dress with
shoulder straps and a drawstring waist. Note the feather-
fringe detail at the hemline, ladies and gentlemen. The skirt
swings flirtatiously with every step, but the garment remains

modest, sophisticated, and structural. A Givenchy classic. Worn by Miss Hepburn in *Breakfast at Tiffany's* during the day but originally intended as a cocktail-hour gown. It's been kept in cold storage since the film wrapped in 1960, so the fabric is pristine and undamaged. Valued at four thousand dollars."

"*Dahling!* That's your dress!" Trina says.

I can't answer. I'm mesmerized by how beautiful it is. "Could you imagine?" I said. "If I had that dress I'd frame it."

"Are you crazy?" Trina says. "A dress like that is meant to be *worn*."

"Four thousand!" Bryan says confidently, raising his paddle.

"Bryan!" I whisper. He just smiles, staring intently at the auctioneer.

"Four five," says a woman in the front row, nodding her head pleasantly. I crane my neck, but all I can see is her pitch-black hair, cropped short, like a pixie cut.

"Thank you," the auctioneer says.

There's a tap on my shoulder. The woman on my left hands me a note and points two seats down. There is Telly, waving.

"Do I have five?" the auctioneer asks.

"Five!" Bryan shouts. He waves his paddle just above his head.

I unfold the note:

Meet me in the ladies'. I have news.

I look over at Telly. Her eyes are bugging out. She means it. But I can't get up now. I shake my head. *Not now.*

"Five five," says the woman in the front row. Most of the people shift in their seats.

"Six!" Bryan shouts. His arm goes up.

The woman in the front row turns and looks back at us. She's wearing reading glasses, which she lowers on her nose. She narrows her eyes at Bryan, then spins back to face the auctioneer.

"Are you crazy?" I whisper.

"It's OK," he mouths. "Don't worry. I won't get stuck with it."

"Six five!"

"Six thousand five hundred dollars," the auctioneer says.

There's a murmur in the crowd. A gray-haired woman in front of us turns around and smiles. "This is getting inter-esting," she says. I'm trying to smile back, but really I'm just gritting my teeth, panicked.

"Do we have seven?"

"Seven," Bryan shouts. I see his face getting red.

I look over at Telly, who's beckoning wildly. I look at the auctioneer, then back at Telly. I shake my head. *Not now!* I have to see what happens.

The pixie cut thrusts her paddle into the air. "Seven five!"

"Eight!" Bryan nearly stands up when he says it.

The crowd stirs again. "Now you're just being annoying," Trina says to Bryan. "You're making me nervous."

"This is fun," he whispers. "I'm OK."

"Eight five!" says the woman in front.

"We have a bid for eight thousand five hundred dollars," the auctioneer says.

"She must really want this thing," Trina says.

The crowd turns toward Bryan, who looks at me, then Trina, then Telly. "Eighty-five hundred dollars!" he mouths.

"Eight thousand five. Do I hear nine?"

"I'm out," Bryan says. He hands Trina his paddle. "I'm sorry, Gemma. I love you and all, but . . . maybe next time."

"I appreciate the thought," I say.

"Let's go find some more of those little sandwiches. That gave me an appetite."

"Great idea."

"Where's Telly?" Trina asks. "Did we lose her?" She smiles and claps her hands, or just her fingers, really, a tiny round of applause.

"Eight five once . . . !" the auctioneer says.

"Be nice," I say. "She's trying." I raise my eyebrows at Trina. "I believe her when she says she's sorry."

Trina sighs. "Oh, you're right, *dahling*," she says. "You always are."

"She's right over there," Bryan whispers. He points to

Telly, who is now standing in the aisle, practically jumping up and down. She holds one hand up, palm facing the front of the room, and points into her palm, gesturing at the row right behind us.

"Eight five twice . . . !"

Before I can turn to see what Telly's pointing at, a voice behind us, a voice that stops me for a second, because I recognize it perfectly, shouts, "Ten!"

I spin around.

Telly was right. She had news.

It's Dusty.

Dusty with the dusty blond hair and the slate-gray eyes. He just bid ten thousand dollars on that dress. He's twice as cute as his profile picture. Maybe three times. And he's smiling straight at me.

ell," Dusty is saying a few minutes later, after the bidding's over and the auctioneer has called for an intermission, "that was exciting."

I'm standing in the aisle talking to him, or, more to the point, listening to him, because I can't believe it's really him. Dusty. Until now, he wasn't real. And I'm still not sure if he is.

Exciting? I think. He just spent ten thousand dollars on a dress. That's more than exciting. That's . . . crazy.

I try not to stare at him, so instead I look down to study

his desert boots intensely, taking in the soft suede, so much cleaner than desert boots should be, as if today's the first day he's worn them. People sweep past us, chattering quietly to one another. I feel them pointing at Dusty.

"Is that the guy who bought the dress?" they're saying. "The one with the fringe? He seems so young. He can't even be twenty years old."

Bryan and Trina are still sitting in their fold-up chairs, bent over like they're in deep conversation. Trina looks over at me and gives me a quick thumbs-up, so quick that I can't tell if she really means it, then she turns back to Bryan. They both look over at me, then go back to talking.

"I like your shoes," I say to Dusty, kicking myself for saying something so stupid.

"Thanks," he says. "And I like yours."

I turn my loafers inward. "What are you doing here?" I ask, looking up at his face. His eyes are soft, gray, like wet stones.

"Same thing you are," he says. He's still smiling.

"Looking at clothes? I thought you hated that stuff."

"I did until I met you," he says.

"You haven't met me yet. I mean, you hadn't met me yet. I mean, we've only just met . . . Oh, you know what I mean." God, I sound like a loser.

"I feel like I've known you for a long time," he says.

I laugh, or it's more like a giggle, and I hope I don't sound too ridiculously nervous. "Did you really just spend ten thousand dollars on a dress?"

"Is that what it was?"

"Um, yes," I say. I can't tell if he's joking or not. But he's smiling, so I smile back. *Ten thousand dollars.*

"Oh," he says, almost shrugging.

"I guess it's not that much," I say, trying to sound . . . what's the word? *Nonchalant.* But I'm sure I just sound snotty. So I say something different. "Between you and me, I have no business being here at all. I mean, I could never afford any of this stuff, not in a million years."

Dusty shrugs his shoulders and looks around the room. He puts his hands in his pockets. "I can't think of anyone who belongs here more," he says. "No one else in the world would appreciate this stuff as much as you do."

"Well, I don't know about that," I say. "There are people who flew in from Japan to be here! And Singapore!"

"Whatever," he says. "Those people are loaded. A transoceanic ride on a private jet means nothing to them. You may have only come from Philly, but you really had to try to get here. You actually earned it."

"I wouldn't say that," I say. "I mean, we crashed it."

"You actually know something about the clothes. About Audrey Hepburn. I should know. I wouldn't have passed my film class if I hadn't met you."

"Maybe so," I say. "But I still don't belong here."

Dusty laughs, and my heart melts hearing the sound of the laughter I've heard so many times over the phone. I know that laugh.

Then again, maybe I don't really know him at all.

"Didn't your boyfriend buy you anything?" Dusty nods his head toward Bryan.

"That's not my boyfriend." I surprise myself at how quickly I say it. "That's—"

I don't need to finish, because suddenly Bryan's standing next to me. "I don't believe we've met," he says, extending his hand to Dusty. "I'm Bryan."

"Dusty," Dusty says, and I look up to see him smile at Bryan. His left front tooth twists almost imperceptibly to the left, but I notice it.

"Of course you are," Bryan says, smiling. "And this is Trina." He points to Trina, standing just behind him.

"Hi," she says. She points her iPhone at Dusty. *Snap*.

There's a nudge at my shoulder. It's Telly, who's just been jostled by a waiter. She leans into my ear. "I told you I had news," she whispers, and pushes past me. "I'm Telly. You must be Dusty. I've heard a lot about you."

I kick Telly.

"Hi," says Dusty. He shakes her hand. "Glad to meet you. I think I've seen your comments on the Tumblr page before."

"Yeah, maybe," Telly says. "But you can ignore those."

Dusty nods. "Fair enough," he says, then he turns to me. "How would you like another glass of champagne, Gemma?"

"Champagne?" I say. I feel like I've had enough already, but I don't want to say so.

"Oh, come on," he says.

"Um, why don't we all get one?" I say. "Why don't we all go? Together." I look at Trina, then Bryan. *Please.*

Bryan shakes his head. "No, you two go ahead," he says. "Trina and I were just saying we both need to visit the restroom, weren't we, Trina?"

"Oh, yes," Trina says.

"Telly, don't you need to use the ladies' room, too?" Bryan's voice is insistent.

"No, I—" Telly says.

"Good, then come along," Bryan says, taking her by the elbow. He turns to me, catches my eye, and winks so quickly I almost don't see it. "We'll come find you in a few minutes." He leans back and whispers in my ear, "Score!" I smack his shoulder.

And, like that, they're gone, disappearing into the milling crowd, all congratulating one another and comparing notes and looking closely at the remaining lots.

"So it's just you and me, then," Dusty says. He takes my hand and leans into the crowd, pulling me behind him. His dark denims and pinstripe blazer make him seem older than what I know him to be—seventeen. "Pardon us, Mr. Koons," he says as he pushes past a handsome man, and "Hello, Ms. Burch," to a blond woman in a pink suit.

"How do you know all these people?" I say.

"From around," he says.

"Just around?" I say.

Dusty flags down a waiter who's walking past with a nearly empty tray. "Is this your last glass?" Dusty asks.

"I'm afraid so, sir," the waiter says.

Dusty offers me the glass.

"No, thanks," I say. "I've had enough. It's all yours."

He takes a sip.

"Just around?" I repeat.

"OK, fine. My mother's last name is Sotheby. I mean, it used to be. Before she married my dad."

My eyes widen. *What?* "Does that mean your family owns Sotheby's?"

"No, we don't own Sotheby's," Dusty says. "Well, not anymore. But I guess we used to. At least, on my mother's side. Long before I was born. Anyway, it does mean that I know a few of these people here. My parents are friends with them. I go to school with their kids."

"I see," I say. "Is it like *Gossip Girl*?"

"Pretty much," he says with a flirty smile. "It also means

I can give the dress back. They'll just sell it to Mrs. LaSalle."

"Who?"

"The woman your boyfriend Bryan was bidding against. She represents a really important collector in Paris. She doesn't want to return empty-handed. She might try to knock a couple Gs off the price, though. You know, since it will have been used." He laughs.

"Bryan's not my boyfriend," I tell him again, and again it comes out almost too quickly. "Bryan doesn't date girls."

"Oh," Dusty says. "Well, whatever."

"What do you mean, 'used'?" I ask.

He doesn't answer, not exactly. Instead he says, "Listen, how long are you in town?"

"Until tomorrow."

"Tomorrow?" Dusty's face sinks, and he pouts out his bottom lip, like a little boy who might throw a tantrum.

"Yeah. Bryan and Trina and I are going to a screening of *Breakfast at Tiffany's* at the Ziegfeld tonight at midnight. Telly, too. We've been planning it for months. And then I catch a train back home in the morning." *Which is the last thing I want to do*, I think. *I want to stay here forever.*

"Oh," Dusty says.

I don't know what he means by that, and so I don't know what to say, exactly, so I change the subject. "Hey, how did you know I was going to be here, anyway?"

"I didn't, until I saw you. I was just here working."

"Working?"

"Well, if you can call a high school internship at the family ex-business working. I just show up a couple of times each week and they let me stick around in case anything happens. So far this summer I've helped one person out to his car. That's it. All they really care about here is that I don't wear sneakers. Best job in the world. I don't get paid, but I get school credit for it."

"Sounds great," I say.

"Like I said, I know some people."

"I see," I say.

"OK, I confess. I wasn't just here working. Didn't you notice? Telly posted a comment on the blog that you'd be here."

I haven't noticed anything on the blog. I haven't even looked at the blog today. I've been a little busy. Did Dusty really see something on the blog, and then decide to come here to find me? I swallow hard and hope I'm not blushing.

"Anyway, I overheard you gushing over that dress earlier in the exhibit room and, well, who else would lose their mind over a dress the way you did in there?"

"I was a little loud, wasn't I?" I say. "I'm sorry."

"It's OK," Dusty says. "It was cute. Anyway, here." He leans over and hands me a slip of paper, folded in half.

"What's this?" I say.

"It's a chit for Lot 14. It's for you."

"Thanks!" I take the paper and turn it over in my hands. "I'll put this in my scrapbook."

"Scrapbook?"

"Yeah, then I'll scan it and put it up on *Oh Yeah, Audrey!* So what are you going to do with the dress, anyway? Are you going to give it back? Or donate it to a museum?"

"It's not just the chit I'm giving you," Dusty says.

I look up at him, searching his slate-gray eyes for an explanation. Surely he's not saying he's giving me the dress. The dress he's just bid ten thousand dollars for. He is giving it back. Isn't he?

"What?"

"Wear it tonight," he says.

"Tonight?" I'm staring at the chit, mesmerized.

"Yes, tonight. You and me. I'm taking you out." He smiles. "There's an art opening in SoHo. We'll have dinner at Josephine. Drinks at a speakeasy in Chelsea, where I know the password. And then Boîte, of course. Have you ever been to Boîte?"

"Dusty, I can't." I look around for Bryan and Trina and Telly. "It, um, it'll never fit."

"Try it on," he says.

"Where?" I say. "Here?"

"Yes," he says. "I can take you to the private suite upstairs."

"Really?" I say. I would like to try it on, at least. That's all. That'll be enough.

"But what about the others?" I say.

"You'll see them tomorrow!"

"I can't just leave them. We have an itinerary. And I can't accept this dress. I can't go with you. It's just not right." *It's just not me.*

"Say yes."

I look at my feet and try to stop my mind from racing. I'm not the kind of girl to ditch my friends and go out with someone I just met. I'm not the kind of girl to be given a gift like this, to be asked out for an evening like this, to wear a dress like this.

But will I ever get another chance like this? I think back on my phone conversations with Dusty and how he made me feel—how I opened up to him, how I told him things I hadn't been able to say to anyone else.

I don't say anything for a minute, or maybe an hour or a second, I'm not sure. So many thoughts clamor for space in my head. I look up at the dress, still on its platform, women gathered around it, sighing.

I think about this day, this incredible day that's only a few hours old. It sweeps before my eyes. Doing my hair in the shared bathroom at the Malcolm. The endless waiting out on the street in front of Tiffany's. Gladiator the bichon frise. Bryan's cognac wingtips. Trina's red updo. Pancakes. The baby grand piano at the Four Seasons. Telly. The dress. The perfect dress with the feathered fringe. The auction. The champagne. Dusty.

"It'll never fit," I say.

"Just try it on," he says.

I look at Dusty. I look at the dress.

Who would I be in that dress?

Maybe I *am* the kind of girl who wears that dress. Maybe all it takes is putting it on to *be* her. To belong.

I turn around to look for Trina and Bryan and Telly. I'm surprised to see them standing right behind me. Telly is tapping on her smartphone. Trina is smiling, but her mouth is tight and I think there's something more to her expression, maybe a look of disappointment. But Bryan's smile is honest, full, and bright.

Dusty leans into my ear as I look over at Bryan and Trina. "Have you ever said yes before?" he whispers.

I don't answer. Bryan looks over at me and nods.

"Say yes," Dusty whispers.

I breathe, turn back to him, and do something that a few minutes ago seemed impossible.

I say yes.

Yes.

'm alone again, staring at myself in the mirror, the massive, ten-foot-high mirror in the marbled bathroom at the Four Seasons, looking at this miraculous dress and wondering how it could possibly fit me so well.

I insisted to Dusty that Bryan had to come with me when I tried on the dress, so Dusty took us upstairs to a room above Sotheby's that was like a little study with a bathroom attached. "Don't worry, I won't look," Bryan said when I stepped out of my picnic dress, even though he was looking. "OK, I'm looking, but I'm not seeing. This is all business. Put your hands up."

He held the dress up over my head, guided my hands through the armholes, and let it drop over my shoulders. The dress, the dress made for Audrey Hepburn by Hubert de Givenchy in 1960, the dress that was older than my mother ever was, slid right over my shoulders and down past my hips. It fit.

"Hmm," Bryan said, holding his finger over his lips, scrutinizing the dress. "Not bad. It's maybe an inch too long, and it's not falling quite as perfectly as I'd like, but—" He zipped up the dress and took a step back.

"But what?" I said, spinning in the mirror.

"But with the right shoes—" he said.

I went up on my tiptoes.

"It will be fabulous."

He was right.

It doesn't fit me as perfectly as it fit Audrey, that's certain. And my shoulders are definitely broader than hers, not as delicate. But I'm in it. The dress fits me. And I'm going to wear it.

I look down at my new shoes, a pair of strappy black heels that Bryan picked out for me at Stuart Weitzman that afternoon. ("My treat," he said. "And my offering to the fashion gods. They'll strike me down if I let you wear that dress with your loafers.") They glisten in the mirror. Bryan was right. The shoes make the dress look even better.

The dress. The perfect black shift with the flirty skirt. The ten-thousand-dollar dress that Audrey Hepburn herself, the most beautiful person ever, made famous. It's impossible.

And yet, there I am in the mirror, standing in the bathroom of an unimaginably glamorous hotel room, wearing an unimaginably glamorous dress, just minutes from an unimaginably glamorous date with an unimaginably charming stranger.

Is this really me?

Stuart Weitzman was only one of our stops. We shopped all afternoon, the four of us, totally ignoring the itinerary. Instead of a walking tour of *Breakfast at Tiffany's* landmarks, we did an SUV tour of uptown's most exclusive stores. Bergdorf's. Bendel's. Barneys.

I, of course, was having a hard time paying attention to anything. I was thinking about my date with Dusty.

Dad texted me again while we were at Barneys. *Hi, Gem. Call when you can.*

"Whatever," I said aloud. I knew exactly what he wanted. He wanted to say he was worried about me, that he wanted me to come home so he knew I was safe. But I don't know. It's more than that. I mean, he was never so protective before Mom died. Sometimes I think all he really wants is just to hang out. To talk. To be with someone because he can't stand being alone.

Can't he just get off my case for one day? Is that too much to ask?

"It's not my responsibility," I said.

Trina heard. "You say something, Gemma?"

"Nothing," I said. "Sorry."

I texted back to Dad: *I'm fine. I'm with my friends.*

What friends?

That's the problem with texting with Dad. As soon as you answer him, it's like he thinks it's an invitation to some kind of text conversation. Which it is not. I was just answering him so he would know that I'm alive, and fine, and that he didn't have to call the cops or send out a search party or anything like that. He could stop worrying about me and leave me alone for a change.

"Are you OK, Gemma?" Bryan asked. "Did you say you wanted to be left alone?"

"Was I talking out loud?" I answered.

"Um, yeah," Trina said.

"Sorry," I said, and I texted to Dad: *I'll call you later.*

"Sorry, guys," I said. "My father's just being—" I shook my head.

"Annoying?" Telly offered, which sounded right.

"Yeah," I said. "Something like that." Only, it was more than that.

"I get it," Trina said. But I'm not sure she really did.

Bryan paid for everything. Trina got a pair of black cigarette pants and a black sleeveless turtleneck pullover. Telly found a crisp white, men's-style button-down shirt and a pair of skinny jeans.

After helping me get ready, the others have now gone over to Seventy-first Street to photograph themselves in front of Holly Golightly's apartment building, so I'm alone in the suite at the Four Seasons, standing in the glass-and-marble bathroom.

"It's not a *date*," I said to Trina just before they left. "I'm just going out with him for a couple of hours. Just for dinner. It's the least I can do after he gave me that dress."

"So you're going out with him as a favor?" she said.

"That's not what I mean. Besides, I'll be back way before the movie."

"I know," she said.

"It's OK, right?"

She paused for a minute, as though she were checking with herself. "Of course it's OK," she said. "I mean, if a guy like that asked me out, I'd go. And seriously, to get to wear that dress? I'd be pissed if you *didn't* go."

"Really?"

She grabbed Telly by the arm. "Do you want to go over

to Holly's apartment and take pictures of ourselves on the steps?" she asked.

"One minute," Telly said, then she leaned into my ear. "Good luck, Gemma. Remember, tonight it's all about you."

"It's all about Audrey," I said.

"No," she whispered. "It's all about Gemma." Then she let Trina drag her toward the door. "We'll be here when you're done!"

"Are you coming?" Trina yelled to Bryan.

"Just a second," Bryan said. He was fussing with my shoulder strap.

"Is Trina mad?" I asked Bryan after the door closed.

"Don't worry about her. She won't even miss you."

"Thanks a lot."

"That's not what I mean," he said. "Gemma, this is huge. *He bought Audrey Hepburn's dress so you could wear it!* Do you really think that any of us would hesitate for a minute if we had the same opportunity?"

"You mean, you'd put on this dress and go out with Dusty if he asked you to?"

"Of course! And you owe it to *us*—to *Oh Yeah, Audrey!*—to wear that dress!"

"I can't believe I'm going out in this, Bryan."

"I can," he said. "It's perfect."

"What if I rip it?" I said. "Or spill something on it?"

"Be brave! And come straight back to the Four Seasons after dinner. You'll tell us everything, and we'll freshen up your makeup, and we'll all go over to the Ziegfeld together."

"Promise?"

"Promise. Your hair looks amazing," he said, adjusting my ponytail.

I curtsied.

"Now, I only have two pieces of advice," Bryan said. "Don't do anything I wouldn't do, and remember, *you're* wearing the dress. The dress isn't wearing you."

"What does that mean?"

"I mean, *own it*, girl! Take that dress out for the night it deserves!"

"I'll try," I said.

"Don't try. Just do it. And Gemma?"

"Yes?"

"Don't be afraid to be swept away. It doesn't happen very often."

Then Bryan kissed me twice, once on each cheek, and left the suite to join the others.

'm standing by the baby grand, looking out at the New York skyline. The sunlight is just starting to go golden. All I can hear is me, breathing.

My phone vibrates. It's a text from my father.

Not now, I think. I ignore it.

A phone on the wall rings. I'm afraid to answer it, afraid it might be Dad. Afraid he might have found me.

It stops ringing, then starts again.

I answer it.

"Gemma Beasley?"

"Yes?"

"This is Rebecca at the front desk. There's a young man here for you." She whispers, as if she's put her hand over her mouth to disguise what she's saying. "And he's cute."

"Thank you," I say, hanging up the phone.

I check my reflection. At least I *think* it's me. One last swipe of lipstick and I grab my phone and hotel key card and step away from the mirror.

I'm not Gemma Beasley.

I'm Holly Golightly.

e pass Tiffany's on the way to SoHo, rounding the corner from Fifty-seventh Street in a big black sedan that isn't exactly a limo but is still bigger than a normal car. I can tell because I can cross my legs.

The New York air is glittering in the silky, honey-colored seven o'clock light. "The magic hour," they call it in the movie business, or at least that's what Bryan said once.

"It was pink this morning," I say quietly, and I wonder if

there's any place more beautiful in the world than Fifth Avenue right now. Probably not.

"What was?" Dusty asks. His hair is pushed back, a couple of strands falling over his forehead: an English schoolboy look. His eyes shimmer, gray and blue and flecks of gold together, sleepy and alive at the same time. "What was pink this morning?"

"Nothing," I say. "Just . . . everything."

"You make me smile," Dusty says, and he does smile. He's wearing slim, stiff denim jeans, a white V-neck T-shirt, and an open tuxedo jacket, and I'm wearing a ten-thousand-dollar dress. I should feel overdressed. But I don't. I feel as glamorous as Audrey Hepburn.

Dusty reaches over and takes my hand, brings it to his lips. He doesn't kiss it, he just holds it there. His lips are soft, and I wonder what it would be like to—

Dusty gives me back my hand, gently placing it on the seat between us. I touch my hair. I can't believe this is happening. *Yes.*

We pass by Tiffany's, and it fades into the city behind us.

he taxi pulls up to the curb next to a sign
that says WYANDOT.

"Is this the restaurant?" I say.

"No," Dusty says. "I just wanted to make
a stop here first. I hope that's all right."

"Where are we?"

"It's his new gallery," Dusty says, point-
ing at the sign. "Larry Wyandot. The Wyandots are the most
important art-dealer family in the city. Maybe the world.
They're hosting an opening tonight for Xi Xi."

"Who?" I say.

"Xi Xi," Dusty says. "He's a Taiwanese painter. His work sells for hundreds of thousands of dollars. Sometimes millions."

"Millions?"

"Millions." He offers his hand as I step out of the car. I've never been around people who can spend millions of dollars before. How should I behave?

"Watch your feet," he says, guiding me over a puddle. His eyes crinkle into a smile.

"Thank you," I say, taking his hand. I see my reflection in the window of the car, and I remember: I'm Holly Golightly. I know exactly how to act.

Inside, the massive, white-walled gallery space is crowded with people. Tall, skinny people with sleek hair and glasses of wine. I feel like I'm entering a room full of supermodels, human beings crossed with spiders, with legs that reach as high as my shoulder. The women wear skirts that are short in the front and long in the back, with turquoise necklaces and silver wrist cuffs. The men wear pastel suits tapered tightly at the ankles, no socks with their loafers.

I don't see any art.

"I thought this was an art gallery."

Dusty just smiles. "Glass of wine?" he asks, his eyes twinkling, gesturing toward the bar at the back of the gallery.

"No, thanks," I say.

"How about a club soda? I mean, you know, sparkling water?"

I accept, and we push our way through the spider people. I watch the floor as I walk, careful not to trip over the maze of elegant shoes. As we approach the back of the room, the crowd begins to thin, and I start to see the art. It's a series of tiny paintings, all of them hung right at waist level.

"That's weird," I say to Dusty, pointing at a group of people bent over in front of a painting. "Kind of makes it hard to see, don't you think?" I can just make out the painting they're admiring, which shows a man divided in two, one side a military uniform, the other side a priest's garb. I wonder what it means.

"Not really," he says. "I mean, no one's really here to look at the art anyway. I mean, a few people obviously pretend to, but that's not really the point of this party."

"Then what are they here for?"

"To look at one another, to see who else is here. To see how they measure up."

"Oh," I say.

"You never know who you're going to run into at a party like this," he says. "For example, look behind you."

"Famous people?" I say. I've never seen anyone famous before.

"Sometimes," he says.

What am I doing here?

I pull out my phone to take a picture of the crowd to send to Bryan and Trina and Telly. There's an alert on the screen, saying I have a text. From Dad. Again. I stare at my phone for a second, but I don't open the text.

"Everything OK?" Dusty asks.

"Yes," I say. "It's nothing." I slip my phone back into my handbag without reading the message or taking a picture. Audrey wouldn't take pictures. Not that she had a smartphone, but still. She'd play it cool. So I'll play it cool. And I'll read Dad's text later.

We wander over to examine a small painting. It's a bird, standing in a tree and looking out over a field, only when you look closer you realize it's not really a bird, it's a girl, bent over and dressed in a jacket of feathers. It's titled *Flying Lessons*.

"I wonder what it means," Dusty says.

But I don't wonder. It's a girl who wants to be something different. Who doesn't think she belongs in the world as a girl. She wants to belong someplace.

"I think it's about—" I start to explain.

Just then, a shock of blond hair swings in front of me, and a young woman materializes from behind it. "Dusty!" she exclaims. "I haven't seen you in forever!" Her eyeliner has a short uptick at the end, like a cat's-eye, but not quite.

"Hey, you." Dusty leans over to kiss her on the cheek. She's wearing a black maxidress and carrying a leather-trimmed chocolate handbag over her forearm.

He takes my hand and gestures at the woman, who is now facing me directly. There's something familiar about her. "Gemma, I'd like you to meet Blake."

I smile nervously and switch my clutch from one hand to the other.

"Hello," I say quietly, trying to figure out where I've seen her before.

"Great dress!" she says to me. "Whose is it?"

I start to point at Dusty, because it takes me a minute to realize she's asking me who designed it, not who *owns* it.

"Oh," I say. "It's vintage."

Dusty wraps his arm around my waist, rescuing me. "Isn't it beautiful?" he says.

"It's so . . . I don't know, it's like something Audrey Hepburn would wear," the woman says, looking down at the skirt. "Oh, my God, is that a feathered fringe? I'm dying, it's gorgeous."

"My Gemma has great taste," Dusty says.

I exhale. *My* Gemma. Like I belong with him. Like I belong here, in New York, at this party, with these people.

"Well, I'm flying out to Barcelona tonight and I still have

to pack!" She turns to me and holds out her hand. "Nice to meet you, Gemma," she says. "Love that dress!"

She kisses Dusty's cheek and saunters toward the door.

"She's beautiful," I say.

"Yes. She is. But so are you."

"Yeah, right!" I say.

"I'm not kidding." His gray eyes dart back and forth, first fixed on my right eye, then my left. He takes my other hand and the rest of the gallery—the spider people, the clinking glasses, the din of conversation—disappears. He holds my fingertips.

"You're *enchanting*," he says.

I freeze. *Enchanting*. It's the magic word.

Enchanting.

Me, Gemma Beasley, who didn't exactly run away from home last night but did leave Philadelphia without so much as telling my father or anyone else there, and who is now wearing one of Audrey Hepburn's dresses in the most exclusive art gallery in New York City, who is being stared at by the most handsome boy I've ever talked to, a boy who's taking me out for a once-in-a-lifetime night in New York City, a boy who thinks I'm enchanting.

This beautiful boy.

I have to go to the ladies' room.

Dusty walks me to it. Inside, I text Trina and Bryan. *OMG, you guys. You won't believe where I am.*

Bryan answers. *Don't tell us, Gem! We want to be surprised. We're going to dinner now. See you soon. #sweptaway*

hat's our next stop?" I ask when we're back outside. *Not that it matters*, I say to myself. It's not like I'm going to object.

"We're headed to NoHo," Dusty says. "It's just a few blocks. I thought maybe we could walk. It's so nice outside."

It really is nice out. It's a warm June evening, with just a little bit of a breeze. There was a swift shower of rain when we were in the gallery and now the air feels fresh. I breathe deeply and I feel like myself again.

"Do you like seafood?" Dusty holds out his hand and I take it, and we walk.

"I *love* seafood," I say.

"Really?"

"Really. I don't know why. My parents hate it. Especially my mom. She can't stand anything fishy, not even shrimp."

"I thought—"

"Yeah. Sorry. That probably seemed weird. Sometimes I talk about her like she's still here. Don't worry, I'm not crazy. I know she's dead."

"Do you miss her?"

"Every day."

"Can I ask you a weird question?"

"Of course."

"Did she ever annoy you?"

He's right. It is a weird question. But he asks it so easily that he makes me want to answer.

"She still does, sometimes," I say. "Like when I'm getting ready for school, and I'm taking a few extra minutes to figure out what shoes to wear, I can hear her in my head sighing and tapping her fingernail on her watch, all 'Hurry up, Gemma, this isn't a fashion show, you know.' Which of course makes me take even longer to get dressed, just to spite her, which is extra stupid because, you know, it's all in my head."

Dusty laughs.

I love being able to joke and be light about this with Dusty. Dad is always so serious whenever we talk about Mom, and I never talk about her with anyone else.

"Tell you what, Gemma, whenever you're in need of an annoying mother fix, I'll just send mine over."

"What's your mother like?"

"Oh, I don't know," he says. "She's kind of flaky. She's cool, I guess. We're pretty good friends."

"Friends?" I say. "How can you be friends with your mother?"

"I know. It's weird, but that's what it's like with us. She acts like she's my age most of the time. But I never really see her that much. She spends most of her time going out or traveling or whatever. I'm never even really sure when she's going to be in town or not. Like tonight, I'm pretty sure she's in Switzerland with her boyfriend."

"Her boyfriend? Your father?"

"No, no. My parents are divorced. Mom got the New York apartment, and she kept his name, too. Doors open when you're a Sant'Angelo, you know."

"I wouldn't know. Nothing happens when you're a Beasley."

Dusty squeezes my hand. "I love Beasleys," he says.

I smile, but I'm not sure I buy it. I wonder if he'd love Beasleys if he really knew who we were. Who I am. A girl who sleeps on a futon because her family can only afford a one-bedroom apartment.

We stop at the corner of a wide boulevard and wait to cross. "Houston Street," I say. "I didn't know we were in Texas."

"It's pronounced *HOW-ston*," Dusty says. "Don't ask me why, because I have no clue."

"Oh," I say. *"HOW-ston."*

We cross quickly, and I start to notice my toes pinching in the tips of my shoes. Not pain, really, but, well, you know the feeling. I'm glad when Dusty slows our pace again on the other side.

"I love summer evenings in New York," Dusty says. "It's so much better here than in London."

"London?"

"That's where my father lives. I usually spend the summers there. Not that I want to, really. I mean, it's nice and all, but New York is . . . New York."

"London. Does your father work with a lot of English musicians or something?"

"Yeah, some. But really, everyone goes to London to record these days." Dusty looks at me. "Wait. How do you know what my father does?"

I shake my head, embarrassed for a moment. "I, um, well, my friend Bryan looked you up. On your Facebook page. He told me. Do you get to meet rock stars all the time?"

"Ha!" Dusty smiles. "Dad doesn't see many of the artists much anymore, except when they come to the office for meetings. He's pretty much an office guy now, dealing with money and contracts and schedules and stuff. Or, I don't know. All I know is he's in that office all day with all those gold records hanging over his head. Literally, on the wall. Someone else does the real musical stuff. At least, that's what it seemed like the last time I went over to visit him, last summer."

"Do you have any brothers and sisters?"

"Nope, just me. Actually, it's just me in the apartment most of the time. Which is weird, because it's a huge apartment."

"That's kind of sad."

"Not really," Dusty says. "I mean, it's not like I'm an orphan. And not only that, I'm a *Sant'Angelo*! You can do anything if you're a Sant'Angelo." I'm not sure, but it sounds like sarcasm in his voice, which makes me feel a little more sad for him.

"Or a Golightly," I say.

"A what?"

"Golightly. Holly Golightly. Holly was the name Audrey Hepburn's character chose when she moved to New York. I don't know if that's the reason doors opened for her, but it was better than Lulamae. At least, she thought so."

"What are you talking about?"

"Holly Golightly, from *Breakfast at Tiffany's*. She ran away from home in Texas, where her name was Lulamae and she was married to this older guy named Doc. But she just knew she didn't belong there, that if she stayed in Texas, her whole life would go by and she would get old and die without ever seeing anything. So she got on a bus one day for New York City, and she picked a new name, found some great clothes, met some fancy people, found an apartment, and the rest is . . . well, she took care of herself. Herself and Cat."

"Cat?"

"That's the name of her cat. Cat."

"Original."

"She said she didn't want to give it a proper name, because it didn't really belong to her. Because no one belongs to anyone else. That's how she felt. Anyway, she took care of herself somehow. She had to get out of her old life and get into a new life and that's how she did it."

"Wasn't her family pissed?"

"Yeah, I think so. Her husband came to find her, but he seemed more hurt than anything, really. Especially when she told him she wasn't going home with him."

"That's kind of harsh."

"I suppose. But you can't just sit and spend your whole life in a place where you don't belong, you know." My mind drifted to an image of my dad, sitting at our kitchen table, waiting for me to come home.

"So how did she pay for herself?"

"She made it work. She met some people."

"People just gave her money?"

I don't want to get too deep into Holly Golightly's cash flow. "Something like that."

"And she wasn't, you know . . ."

"What?"

"Did men give her money for . . ."

"She wasn't a prostitute, if that's what you mean. Although she did talk about going on dates with men who would give her fifty dollars for the powder room. I prefer to think they just paid her for her company."

"Sounds kind of fishy to me," Dusty says.

I don't know how to answer.

And Dusty doesn't say anything for a few moments, either. "Well, whatever you call it, it sounds pretty impressive. To make it in New York City without a real job and everything. And for men to give you money for—just for going to the bathroom. I guess that's a pretty sweet deal."

"Haven't you ever seen *Breakfast at Tiffany's*?"

"Would you still have gone out with me if I hadn't?"

I laugh.

"Don't answer that," Dusty says, and quickens his pace. "The restaurant's just up here on the left. I'm starving."

e walk into a restaurant, a huge, bustling bistro with low booths and mirrors all around. The room is full of soft, sparkling light, bouncing from the overhead chandeliers. People sit in small groups over glasses of wine, laughing and toasting one another.

"It's called Josephine," Dusty says.

"Josephine," I repeat.

"Yeah, it's pretty popular these days. It's not easy to get a table here at the last minute, so I hope they have room for us."

Dusty approaches the host stand, where a handsome man with a closely cropped gray-and-white beard, wearing a white shirt and black tie, says, "Reservation?"

"We don't have one," Dusty says. "But we'd like a table for two, please."

"I'm sorry, we don't have anything," says the man. He starts tapping into his computer. "If you want to wait, we'll have something at, let me see—"

"No, we'd like to sit *now*, please," Dusty says, his voice rising. I can feel tension from the host.

"Sir, we are completely—"

"Do you know who I am?" Dusty snarls. "*Sir?*"

"I—"

Dusty leans over and whispers into the host's ear. I look around and smile stupidly at the couple standing behind us, feeling uncomfortable.

The host jerks his head back and his eyes widen. "Of course, Mr. *Sant'Angelo*," he says. He smiles at me and holds out his hand. "Right this way, please."

Dusty shakes his head and gestures for me to follow the host. "Go," he says gruffly.

I go, shoulders stiff.

The host takes us immediately to a corner table next to the front window. He signals to a busboy, who rushes over with water.

"Mademoiselle," Dusty says as I take a seat with my back to the wall.

"What did you say to him?" I whisper as I sit.

"I just reminded him what would happen to him if he didn't seat us right away." He smiles, just this side of sinister. "Don't worry," he says, and his face softens back to normal, slate-gray eyes sparkling. "I just want tonight to be perfect. For you."

My stomach turns as he says this, but I decide to let it go. Until then, the evening has been perfect. I exhale, take a sip of water, and pretend to read the menu, which is in French, which means I can't actually read it, but I still pretend to.

When the waiter comes over and introduces himself as Claude, pronouncing it *Cloood*, I'm relieved when Dusty offers to order for us.

"We'll have the *tour des fruits de mer*," he says, sounding Parisian.

"Very good," the waiter says.

The *tour* is a three-tiered platter of shrimp, crab, smoked mussels, and raw oysters, piled over crushed ice and seaweed. Little silver dishes of cocktail sauce and shallot vinegar are nestled in, too, and slices of lemon wrapped in green gauze. Dusty spritzes the oysters with lemon and picks one up. "To you," he says, toasting me with it.

I click my oyster shell on his and, together, we slurp.

We devour the tour, matching each other oyster for oyster, shrimp for shrimp, crab leg for crab leg, locking eyes and laughing. It's the most delicious thing I've ever tasted.

Next, the waiter brings over two plates of steak with salty, thin French fries. Dusty asks if I'd like a glass of wine and I say no, thanks, so he orders two glasses of sparkling water instead.

"You know what it is about her?" he says, as he slices his way through another morsel of steak.

"What are you talking about?" I've eaten all of my French fries already and haven't even touched my steak yet. "About who?"

"Audrey Hepburn. I mean, what was her name again? In the movie?"

"Holly Golightly."

"Yeah. I think I know what it is about her that makes people like her. Makes *you* like her so much."

"You mean, besides the fact that she was incredibly beautiful and completely charming and had the most amazing clothes?"

"Yeah, besides that. Look, Gemma, I don't think being beautiful and having great clothes is all that special. Look around! There are beautiful people all over this room and none of them seem all that special to me."

"I don't know," I say. "Maybe they are special."

"But are any of them as special as Audrey Hepburn? I mean, Holly Golightly? If you ask me, it sounds like she had something more. Like she could make things happen."

"How do you mean?"

"She just seems to know how to get things done. She wasn't waiting for someone else to take care of her. If she'd wanted that, she would have stayed home in Texas. But she said screw it, I'm out of here, even though things would be hard and she'd have to take care of herself. And she did. She handled things her way. I admire that."

It's probably the most words I've ever heard Dusty say all at once, and the way they fall out of him, it's like he means them. Which makes me really like him.

Or maybe I should say: Which makes me finally admit that I really like him.

I catch my reflection in one of the mirrors. My shoulder strap is turned over, so I straighten it.

"That reminds me of you. You make things happen. You got yourself here."

It just might be the best compliment I've had all day.

I ask him where the ladies' room is. He points to the back of the restaurant. "I don't have fifty dollars on me, though," he says. "Unless you accept debit cards." He smiles.

"Funny," I say as I stand up, and I can't help smiling back.

While I'm gone he orders a plate of profiteroles—little pastries with ice cream and chocolate sauce drizzled over the top. Before we eat them, I take a picture and send it to Bryan, Trina, and Telly.

ryan: *That dessert looks amazing. When are you going to be done with dinner?*

Me: *Maybe, like, 45 minutes?*

Bryan: *That means an hour in New York time.*

Me: *I'm sorry. I didn't know this was going to take so long.*

Bryan: *It's OK. We just finished dinner at 21 Club. See you when we see you.*

s it OK? I really want to show you this place," Dusty
says. "We'll just stop in for a minute."

I look at my watch. "OK," I say. Bryan and Trina
will be fine.

"It's on the roof," Dusty says as we pass the
eleventh floor in the elevator. "Sort of." We're in
a building a short car ride from the restaurant,
in a neighborhood Dusty told me is called Chelsea. There
were a few cabs on the street when we got out, but it's not as
crowded as SoHo.

"What do you mean, 'sort of' on the roof?"

"You'll see."

We exit the elevator at sixteen, and Dusty leads me down a deserted hallway with peeling paint to a door with a big sign saying DO NOT USE EXCEPT IN CASE OF FIRE. ALARM WILL SOUND!

"Push it." He smiles.

"What? The alarm will go off!"

"Have you ever set off an alarm before?" he says. And so I scrunch up my shoulders and push.

Nothing. Not a sound.

We walk out onto the roof, and the city is sparkling around us. In the distance, I can see the Empire State Building lit up in red, white, and blue. I can hear, faintly, what sounds like a guitar and several people singing, but I don't see any party.

"Are you sure this is the right roof?" I ask.

"I'm sure." Dusty leads me across the roof toward a water tower. I hear the music getting louder.

"We're here," Dusty says.

"We're where?"

He points to the water tower. "The party's in there."

"What?"

"I was here last week," Dusty says. "You're not going to believe it. It's, like, the ultimate speakeasy. Who needs a secret party in a basement, when these guys throw a secret party in a water tower!"

"Isn't that kind of wet?" I ask, hoping my sarcasm covers up my anxiety.

"Good one, Gem. No, the water tower has been emptied and refilled with people. Hipsters! With suspenders and mustaches. And girls with feathers in their hair."

"How do you get in there?"

He points to a ladder leading up to a small opening that's been cut out of the side of the water tower. Through it, I can see feet, and light flickering between them.

I shake my head.

"What?"

"I hate heights."

"Don't worry. The ladder is secure. It's bolted into the tower. And I'll be right behind you to catch you."

"My dress," I say. "I mean, your dress. It'll rip on the ladder."

"Come on. Do you think Holly would have skipped a party in a water tower on a roof in New York City because she didn't want to tear her skirt?" He stands behind me and corrals me toward the ladder. "You'll be fine. I'm here."

He has a point. I hike up my skirt and start climbing, being careful not to look down.

"You found it, homie!" says a guy in suspenders and a fedora as we crawl into the water tower. "This must be Gemma."

I look over at Dusty.

He answers my question before I can ask it. "I told him

you were coming," he says. "I told them I was bringing the coolest girl on the planet. Derek Blackbird, meet Gemma Beasley."

"Charmed," says Suspenders.

I'm charmed, too. It's like magic up here.

We are in a tiny round room with a very high ceiling. Built into the walls are shelves lined with bottles of liquor. A small bar has been constructed off to one side, and on it stands a tattooed woman. She is singing in French; I don't understand the words, but the sounds are sad. Next to her stands a guy with a guitar. Surrounding them are about twenty people, men with waxed mustaches and women with loose ponytails and dresses cinched tightly at the waist. They're crowded into the room, if you can call it a room. They're chatting, flirting, swaying with smiles on their faces, even though the song sounds so sad.

Dusty hands me a glass of something. I sip it, but it tastes bitter. "It's called absinthe," he says. "Sip it slowly."

"Did you know you're breaking the law, Gemma?" Derek Blackbird says.

"What?" I turn around to Dusty. "What is he talking about?" I hold out my glass to Dusty.

"This whole party, the whole thing, is illegal," he says, pushing my glass back to me. "We're all trespassing. We could go to jail. All of us."

"But how did they do all the construction and everything in here, if it's illegal?" I ask.

"Isn't it great?" he says. He leans over to whisper in my ear. "You're a beautiful outlaw, Holly Golightly."

My eyes dart around the room. Everyone here seems so perfect. This feels so harmless. How could this be illegal? I picture myself being arrested, riding in the back of a squad car to a police station, and calling my father, explaining to him that yes, I am in New York City, and yes, I'm with a strange boy, and yes, I was picked up at an illegal party in an abandoned water tower on the roof of a building. I close my eyes for a second and remember. I'm not myself, I'm Holly Golightly. She would stay here.

"Don't worry," Dusty says. "I'll take care of you."

"Great dress!" says the singer. Everyone turns to look at me, nodding in agreement.

I smile dumbly. The music starts back up, this time a happier tune, a bouncy melody that everyone seems to know the words to. A few of the partygoers form a circle, and a bald guy with a beard and knickers gets in the middle, dancing a little jig while the others clap. I sway back and forth, and Dusty sways with me. Soon he's spinning into the center of the circle, trying to imitate the bald guy's jig. I laugh and pull out my phone to take a picture.

It's after ten. I need to text Bryan and Trina, so I write:

You won't believe where I am. I tap the camera button and try to frame a shot of the room, but I can't capture it all in one frame.

Derek Blackbird taps me on the shoulder. He's shaking his finger at me. "No phones. And especially no pictures!"

"Sorry," I say, putting my phone into my bag.

"Did you erase it?"

"What?"

"I need to see you erase it. I'm sorry."

I take my phone out and erase the photo. I'm half-embarrassed, half-annoyed. Maybe a little bit more embarrassed than annoyed.

Dusty skips over to me. He picks up my glass, takes a sip, and hands it to me. I sip, too, finishing it. He takes my hands and backs his way to the center of the ring, bringing me along with him.

And we dance.

climb back down the ladder out of the water tower, carefully hiking my skirt over my knees and balancing on the rungs in my strappy slingbacks. The ten thousand dollars' worth of jersey squeezes my chest, pressing the air out of my lungs. I can't fall. I can't tear this dress. But I need to hurry.

The ladder rungs feel sturdy, except for the second to last, which wobbles under my foot. I make it down safely, and so does the dress. I smooth out the skirt and exhale, relieved.

Dusty sticks his head out of the opening at the top of the

ladder. "I'll be right there. I just need to tip the music guys."

I walk to the edge of the roof and look down onto the traffic below. Yellow taxis and black town cars crawl by on the street in bursts of speed, then abrupt halts. I wonder where they're all going.

A breeze blows through the buildings and across my shoulders. I shiver and I inhale, and it feels good. This is what it's like to be in New York. To belong in New York. This is how Holly felt.

My phone vibrates. It's a text from my father: *Where are you? You said you'd call.*

I'm not sure how to answer, so I don't.

Instead, I send a text to Bryan. *New York is so magical.*

We miss you.

I'm sorry. I promise I'll be there soon.

OK, Gemma. We are going to leave here at 11. Do you want to meet us at the Ziegfeld?

No, I'll meet you at the hotel.

Back down at the car, I slide into the seat next to Dusty. He leans over, like he might kiss me, but I turn my head and look out the window, pretending not to see.

"Mind if we make one more stop before I take you back?" he asks, leaning back into his seat. "There's a place you just have to see."

I'm so tempted. Everything he's shown me tonight has been so magical. Unlike anything I've ever experienced before.

"I wish there was more time, but I promised my friends I'd be back right after dinner."

"You've already broken that promise," Dusty says, pointing at his watch. I don't like the way it sounds, like he's accusing me.

"But that's because—"

"Besides, how close friends are they really? Didn't you just meet them, like, today?"

I just look out the window.

"Aren't you having fun?" he says.

"Of course I am," I say, and I mean it. Dusty's completely charming. New York is dazzling. I'm in a dress that belonged to Audrey Hepburn, out on the town with an impossibly handsome, ridiculously rich guy. The kind of guy everyone in the world tells you is perfect. But I feel conflicted.

"You won't believe this place," Dusty says. "You're going to love it."

"Can you take me to the Ziegfeld right afterward?"

"This is the last stop, I promise," he says. He takes my hand, palm up, and kisses the inside of my wrist. His gray eyes crinkle into a smile and bore into mine. He is irresistible. "Say yes?"

I don't say yes. I don't say anything, but we both know that doesn't mean no.

Dusty takes out his phone.

"Hey, Franco! It's Dusty."

re you sure this is it?" I say when the cab stops. We've pulled up to what looks like a dingy warehouse, with no streetlights or businesses anywhere around.

"Yes," he says. "It's right around the corner." He takes my hand and helps me out of the cab. He hands the driver a twenty and we walk. There's a doorway with a single lightbulb hanging over it and a tall, bald doorman in platform shoes and huge fake eyelashes standing out front. At least I think it's a man. A line of people is pressed up against the building waiting to get in.

It snakes all the way down the street, with cigarette smoke hanging over it like a fog.

Dusty leads me to the front of the line and whispers something to the doorman. The doorman steps aside and Dusty nudges me forward. "Franco, this is Holly," he says.

"Charmed," Franco says dully. He pushes open the door, and loud, thumping music spills out into the street. Dusty leads me inside.

"Where are we?" I yell over the loud music.

"Boîte!"

"What?" I yell back.

"Boîte! It means 'box' in French! As in, look at all these people stuffed into this box! Can you believe it's in this neighborhood?"

Actually, I have no idea what neighborhood we're in. And it's hardly a box. It's a large room with a big square dance floor in the middle, surrounded by high walls with balconies overlooking the floor. The balconies are filled with people hanging their feet over the edge, swinging to the loud, throbbing dance music. A small stage stands at the front of the room, with a spotlight on it but no one there. As my eyes adjust to the light, flashing with colors and strobes, I can only see heads and shoulders and torsos bouncing up and down throughout the room.

I feel awkward. This dress does not belong in this club.

"Come on, *Holly!*" Dusty yells. "Don't you like to dance?"

That's all the warning I have before he drags me into the middle of the dance floor, bouncing as he goes. It's uncomfortable in the middle of the crowd, and I keep getting bumped and jostled as I look around, spinning gawkily in my slingbacks.

There must be hundreds of people here, so many more than at the last party, and they're spinning and swaying and posing. A huge mirror ball hangs directly above Dusty and me, sending beams of glittery light in every direction. There's no room to actually dance, of course, but I try to keep moving with Dusty while I stare at the people around me. There are guys in full makeup and platform shoes. Girls in tight jeans and tank tops. A guy in a top hat and tails. A pair of girls in matching satin bubble skirts with slick spit curls of hair pasted to their foreheads. Someone wearing a lizard mask. A woman with a feather boa around her head. Or is it *his* head?

The song morphs into another song, and Dusty stops dancing. "Let's get a drink!" he yells, and we bounce over to the bar.

We have a moment to breathe. Dusty orders himself a vodka tonic and one for me, too. I hate the taste of it, so I pretend to drink. Dusty downs his and orders another. I can't believe how easy it is to get a drink. I can't believe we're here in the first place. No one even asked us for ID.

I check my phone. There's a text from Telly. *We're heading to the Ziegfeld.*

My stomach jumps. They're on their way to the main event, the whole point of this weekend, this weekend I've been looking forward to forever, and they're going without me. The flashing lights and the crushing crowd and the music swirl around me, but all I can think of is my friends waiting for me.

I show Dusty the text.

"Don't worry," he says. "I'll get you to the theater in time. I promise."

I believe him.

I text Telly back. *I'll be there.*

I hope it's true.

he man in the top hat and tails steps into the spotlight. "Ladies and gentlemen!" he announces.

"Showtime!" Dusty says. "Come on." He grabs my wrist and pushes through the crowd to the back of the room, where a velvet rope hangs in front of a doorway. A large, muscular man in a sailor hat stands next to it.

"Is this VIP?" Dusty asks the man.

"You are . . . ?"

"Are you kidding?" Dusty says.

"No," the burly man says.

"Dusty Sant'Angelo," Dusty says.

The man unclips the velvet rope.

"Idiot," Dusty mutters.

"Huh?" I say.

"Not you," he says. "You're perfect." We slip through past the bouncer and up the stairs.

We sit on the edge of the balcony that surrounds the dance floor, our arms draped over the lower rung of the railing. I take off my shoes so they don't land on someone underneath us. We have a perfect view of the stage from up here. Dusty puts his arm around my shoulder and says the magic words: "You're enchanting."

His slate-gray eyes are smiling at the same time, and I am amazed, again, by his beauty.

Enchanted.

I inhale but don't answer. I look down onto the crowd.

He leans toward me, his lips so close I can feel them graze my ear. "Gem," he whispers.

I turn to him, thinking he'll pull his head back. But he doesn't. He's so close I have to dart my eyes from one of his eyes to the other. Each beautiful, slate-gray eye.

"Can I kiss you?" he says, or breathes, and I feel his voice on my face.

I don't have time to answer. He reaches up, stroking my cheek with his hand.

"I've been thinking about this since I first saw you today," he whispers. His breath is sweet and warm. "No, even longer than that. I've wanted to kiss you since that first night on the phone, Gem."

I close my eyes and let myself be swept away.

P lease welcome . . . the Licorice Twins!" the man in the top hat booms.

The pair of women in the bubble skirts emerge from behind the curtain. A ragtime piano song starts, and one woman raises her leg straight up past her shoulder and puts her heel on the other's shoulder. Then her partner does the same, flashing a wicked look at the audience as she does it. They stand, each on one leg, facing each other, and wiggle their toes, shimmying closer to each other until they look like one long vertical line. Then they both blow huge bubbles with gum, pressing the bubbles into each other so that they distort and move but don't pop. They bend and contort without breaking their giant bubbles, and the crowd applauds. I've never seen anything like it. It's creepy and beautiful all at the same time.

I lean over to Dusty. "Do you think they're handsomely paid?"

It's paraphrasing a line that Holly Golightly said to Paul Varjak in *Breakfast at Tiffany's*, but Dusty doesn't get it. Instead he just winks.

The crowd cheers again. And Dusty whistles.

I cheer, too.

The show ends as quickly as it began.

I check my phone. There's a text from Bryan. *We're in row M. Are you coming?* it says.

"I have to go," I say. I point to my watch. "I have to go *now*."

Dusty turns toward me. "Are you sure?" he says. He leans over and kisses me again.

Jelly texts. *Are you OK? We are worried.*

I don't answer.

rina texts. *Where the hell are you?*

I don't answer.

y stomach crawls up underneath my throat when I realize that I've missed the start of the movie. It's not a surprise, exactly. Of course I've seen this moment coming for a while now. But now it's here, and I can't believe it. I can't believe where I am.

I'm in the middle of the most exciting date of my life, and I'm furious with myself at the same time. I think of Bryan and Trina snuggled into their chairs at the Ziegfeld, an empty seat between them. It's a bewildering mixture of feelings, and having them makes me feel dizzy.

"Let's get a drink," Dusty says, and I follow him downstairs to the bar. I've already broken my promise to my friends.

I've chosen Dusty.

 usty and I are standing on Fifty-seventh Street, just down from the Four Seasons, and Dusty is saying good night. He hugs me, and just as my chin finds his shoulder, Bryan, Trina, and Telly walk by, and my heart drops to the sidewalk.

I know they see me, and I know they hear when I say, "Hey, you guys," but they keep walking. Bryan nods as he goes, and Telly looks at me and then looks down. Trina doesn't even look up.

"What is it?" Dusty says, releasing me.

I point to my friends, walking up the steps into the hotel.

Neither of us says anything for a minute.

Dusty offers, "You can stay at my place, Gemma." He takes one of my hands between his, holding it gently, trying to find my eyes with his.

I look away.

"If you don't want to go back to the Four Seasons, I mean."

But I do want to go back to the Four Seasons. I want to run up the stairs and take off this dress and sit with my friends in the hotel room. I want to sip coffee with them and stay up late and tell one another about our evening. I want everything to be just like it was before.

But everything is different now. And it's my fault.

I know I should go after Bryan and Trina and Telly right now. I know I should thank Dusty for my magical evening, promise to return the dress in the morning, and run after them. And ask them to forgive me. That's what Gemma Beasley from Philadelphia, Pennsylvania, would do.

Or would she?

Maybe I'm just scared of what they'll say to me, of what they think of me now.

I talk myself into believing that if I give them a couple of hours to sleep it off, they'll have an easier time forgiving me.

I talk myself into believing that they are the mean ones, for ignoring me just now. I would never do that. Would I?

What would Holly Golightly do?

What would Audrey Hepburn do?

What would Gemma Beasley do?

I don't know who's who anymore.

I watch my three friends walk up the steps to the Four Seasons. I wonder if one of them will turn around and look for me. If just one of them does, I'll break free from Dusty's hands and follow them. I swear I will.

But they don't turn around. It's like I don't even exist.

"I'll take care of you," Dusty says softly, leaning into my ear. He takes my cheek in one hand, his fingers surrounding my chin, his other arm around my waist, like a life raft. "Don't worry. They'll get over it in the morning."

"All right," I say, to Dusty and to myself. I wonder if my room at the Malcolm is still empty, waiting for me. Shouldn't I just go there? But then I look into Dusty's eyes.

"I'll stay with you tonight."

Shh!" I say when Dusty slams the door behind us.

"Oh, don't worry," he says. "No one's home. Even if they were, they wouldn't care."

"They don't care if you bring home a girl from a nightclub at two o'clock in the morning?"

"Three o'clock," he says. "And, no."

"You mean it happens all the time?"

"No. I mean, they'd probably just assume it's one of my

buddies from school or something. I don't know. I've never brought anyone home in the middle of the night before."

"Sure," I say skeptically.

He takes my hand and kisses it. "Really."

I take my hand back and fiddle with my purse.

"Come to my room," he says and leads me down a wide hallway. We pass by a couple of closed doors and a wide entrance to a large living room with a fireplace. We pass a bathroom. "Excuse me," I say. I duck into it and close the door.

I turn on the water and look around the huge, white-tiled room. Behind me is a massive bathtub with feet that look like lions' paws. The toilet is in a separate little closet beyond that. I rinse my hands under the water and smooth down my ponytail. I take a white towel off the huge stack and wipe my hands dry, then hang it from the silver rack to my right.

I didn't think places like this existed in New York City. But Dusty's family is, of course, rich. Very rich.

Dusty's standing in the hallway when I open the door.

"Do you have a guest room or something?" I say.

"You can stay in my room," he says.

"No, that's OK. I'd really rather—I mean, I could stay on the couch or something."

"No way," he says. "You're staying with me." He takes my hand again and we walk to the far end of the hallway. "In here."

He pushes the door open into a big room, very big. Much bigger than any bedroom I've ever been in before, with a row of windows looking out onto the flickering city.

The room doesn't have that much stuff in it. Just a couple of dressers and a big easy chair and a flat-screen television on the wall. And a bed.

It's a big bed, really high off the ground like the kind rich people have, at least in my imagination. Like one of those huge beds where, if you wanted to, you could have the whole family lying on it and all the dogs and everything, too. Not like the thin mattress Dad sleeps on, the one he shared with Mom before she died.

There are piles of clothes on the floor. I wonder if some of them are clean, and if some of them are dirty, and whether he has some kind of system to tell which is which. The clothes are like leaf piles on a lawn during the autumn, and I wonder what it would be like to take a flying leap off the tall four-poster bed and land in one of them. I wonder if these are all the clothes he has or if the dressers and closets (I can count two) are full of clothes, too.

He sits down on the easy chair. "Hey," he says.

"What?"

"Are you OK?"

"What do you mean?"

"I mean, you've hardly said a word since you saw your friends outside the Four Seasons," he says.

"What am I supposed to say?" I ask.

"I don't know," he says. "You've been surprising me all night with the things you say. But now you seem so far away."

I have a thought, that if we were talking on the phone right now, I might open up to him, tell him how I really feel, that I made a huge mistake, that I should have stayed with my friends, that I feel like a jerk for letting him and the dress distract me from why I was in New York City in the first place. That I didn't know what I was doing here in his room. That I didn't know who I was. That I really, really missed my mother. And wished I could tell her everything right now. Maybe she would understand.

"I'm sorry," I say, and as soon as I say it, I realize how weak and small I sound.

"Come on, Holly Golightly," he says, sitting on the edge of the bed and patting it with his hand. "Come sit next to me."

But instead I walk around to the other side of the bed and hoist myself up onto it. My feet must be three feet off the floor. I undo the straps on my shoes and let them fall to the ground. I lie down, curling my feet underneath myself, and turn away from him, as close to the edge of the bed as I can.

I feel his hand on my shoulder. "Come on, Holly," he says again. I feel his finger run underneath the edge of my dress, underneath the strap of my bra. I pretend I have an itch on my shoulder and squirm away from him.

"It's been such a good night, hasn't it? Don't ruin it now. Can't we—"

I can feel his breath on the back of my neck, and it's warm, too warm, almost hot, and I want to roll right off the bed and fall onto the floor. I feel his hand on my hip. I curl my feet more tightly underneath me. Dusty's lips are on my neck, kissing me. I feel his body curling around mine, his hands around my waist, drawing up toward my chest.

"Stop," I say.

"But, Gemma . . ."

"I can't," I say.

"What do you mean you can't?" he says. "You can. *We* can."

"Dusty," I say, and I push his hand away.

"Come on, Holly," he says. "I thought we had a connection."

He's right. We did have a connection. All those hours on the phone, when he seemed like he understood me. All the fantastic places he brought me tonight, when he seemed like he cared. Now everything feels different.

"I bought you the dress. I showed you a good time." He unbuttons his shirt and puts my hand on his stomach. "Now it's your turn."

I pull my hand away. "It is *not* my turn."

It feels so good to say that. I slide off the bed and onto my feet.

"What are you doing?" He sits up on the bed. "Where are you going?"

"I'm leaving."

"You can't go," he says, reaching out for my arm. "You said you'd stay with me."

"I changed my mind," I say. I jerk my arm away from him and pick up my shoes off the floor. I bend over and start to strap them on, but they're too hard to fasten when I'm standing up. *Forget it.* I'll walk out barefoot.

Dusty falls back onto the bed and sighs. "Can I ask you a question before you go?" he says. *"Holly?"*

I don't answer, hoping he won't keep talking. I move toward the door.

"Why did you say yes?"

"I didn't say yes," I say.

"Yes, you did. You said yes when I gave you the dress. You said yes when I asked you out. You said yes when I kissed you. You said yes."

I reach up to feel my hair in the dark. My ponytail is loose now, not sleek and tight like it was last night, but sloppy. I can feel tendrils of hair on my neck. I try to tighten it, but I just catch it in my rubber band, tearing my hair. I look at him, lying there on the bed, not nearly as beautiful as he was a few hours ago.

"I made a mistake." I reach the door and step across the threshold and into the hallway, with my shoes hanging from my finger. "And another thing."

"What?" Dusty asks.

"I'm not Holly."

Before I can close the door to his bedroom, Dusty jumps up off the bed. He grabs his wallet from his dresser. "Here!" he yells, holding out a fistful of cash. "Here's your fifty dollars for the powder room. Isn't that what girls like you expect for your company? *Gemma?*"

I slam the door and run down the hallway to the front door, the elevator, freedom.

'm not sure what part of town I'm in. I see a clock through a diner window, and it tells me I've been wandering around for an hour, maybe more. It'll be morning soon, something I'm not sure I'm happy about. It'll be the second morning in a row that I'm wearing an Audrey Hepburn dress before dawn. Only this time, it really *is* an Audrey Hepburn dress, not a fake from a secondhand store. A real dress that she actually wore. But I couldn't feel more like a fraud.

I shiver in the cool air and my feet are killing me. I stop and balance my clutch on the rim of a garbage can, then crouch down to slip on my heels. But my butt knocks into my clutch, which goes tumbling into the garbage can just as I slip my toe into my shoe.

"Crap," I say. "What is wrong with you? Can't you put on your shoes without throwing your bag in the garbage?"

A man walking toward me hears me, I guess, and crosses over to the other side of the street. I realize I'm talking to myself again. I'm alone in the street, at four in the morning, trying to put my shoes on, and I've just knocked my purse into a garbage can and I'm talking to myself.

I lean over and reach in to grab my clutch, but I lose my balance and teeter over sideways, nearly falling into the garbage can myself. *How perfect,* flashes through my mind.

I try to catch myself on the edge of the garbage can, lifting one foot up to regain my balance. I feel my heel catch in the dress just as I try to steady myself.

I sprawl to the sidewalk with a loud rip. It's not me ripping, it's the dress, and it's the loudest noise I've heard all night. Louder than the music at Boîte. It's the sound of a ten-thousand-dollar, one-of-a-kind, vintage Hubert de Givenchy dress, once owned by Audrey Hepburn, the most wonderful person and most glamorous movie star who ever lived, being torn to shreds. It sounds like a jet tearing through the sky. Like a page ripping from a book. Like a car screeching around a corner when it should have stopped at the light instead.

I can't believe this. I've put the heel of my shoe right into the seam where the feather-fringed hem starts. I've torn Audrey Hepburn's dress.

I watch as a couple of strands of feathery fringe waft away, into the deserted street.

4:30 A.M.

'm still sitting on the sidewalk, watching the feathers float away, so tired, so defeated, when I remember the unanswered texts on my phone from my father.

I want to ignore them. I want him to leave me alone. Just for a weekend, is that too much to ask?

I look at my scuffed shoes, twist a piece of feathered fringe in my fingers. And it hits me: Dad is the only person left who actually cares about me. And what kind of daughter doesn't call her dad to let him know that she's OK when he's already lost the other most important person to him? He'll probably never forgive me after the stunt I pulled this weekend, and for what?

Trina and Bryan don't care about me anymore, that's for sure. And who can blame them? I ditched them on what was supposed to be the greatest weekend of our lives.

Telly doesn't care about me. Why should she? Telly was the only one who saw Audrey Hepburn as more than just a beautiful, talented movie star. Unlike me or Bryan or Trina, Telly fell in love with Audrey Hepburn for the right reasons. For her compassion. For her charity. For the person she was inside, not because of what she looked like. For *being there*. Telly saw things more clearly than I ever did.

Tonight it's all about you, she'd said. *It's all about Gemma.*

And I've blown her off, too.

I've pushed everyone away—even myself—by pretending to be Audrey Hepburn or Holly Golightly or I don't even know who, wearing someone else's dress in someone else's city, living someone else's life. And now I'm here, on the cold sidewalk, with mascara streaks on my face and a torn dress. Too ashamed to call my dad, too ashamed to call my friends.

And it's my fault.

Telly was right. It *is* all about me.

When are you going to figure out who you really are, Gemma?

4:35 A.M.

I'm on Park Avenue, I think. At least it looks like Park Avenue, this canyon of big shiny buildings, just like where Holly told Paul how much she loved New York, even though she was leaving to marry José the Brazilian.

The sidewalk is mostly deserted, just some taxis heading toward Grand Central Station, taking early-morning people and late-night people to the trains, which in turn will take them where they need to be. Work, maybe, or home.

Home.

It's gray and wet this morning—not raining, just . . . wet.

My phone vibrates through my clutch. It's a text from Dusty.

I need the dress back. It doesn't belong to you.

I don't answer. I wouldn't really know what to say to him anyway. The dress is ruined.

I've never felt so alone. I want to go back to the Four Seasons, find my friends and crawl into bed, and just pretend it's yesterday again.

Maybe I'll just keep walking, past Grand Central and through midtown to Penn Station, and get a train back to Philadelphia. I don't need all my stuff at the hotel. I can do without it. I think there's a train to Philadelphia every hour. I can be back to the apartment by nine o'clock. I could buy a hoodie at the station for the ride home, one of those cheap NYPD ones they sell to tourists. No one would think anything about a scraggly girl in a torn dress and a tourist hoodie on the morning train to Philadelphia. They'd just think . . . I don't know. They'd just think I was the kind of girl who takes the train alone in a torn dress and a disheveled ponytail, after a night out partying with men who give her fifty dollars for the powder room.

Maybe I am that kind of girl. This isn't Audrey Hepburn's life. This is mine.

I wander up and down Seventy-first Street, trying to find Holly Golightly's building. But in the darkness I can't tell which one it is.

There's scaffolding over some of them, and I can't see the striped awning and red stairs that Holly's apartment had. I cross the street and go one block farther. I still can't see it. I double back. All the buildings look the same, bricks and stair railings and ivy-covered walls. I'm not even sure if I'm heading east or west.

I feel a little dizzy. My feet hurt. I'm hurt.

I sit down on a stoop, just to give my feet a rest.

I slip off my slingbacks and am rubbing my heels when I look up the stoop. There are the striped awnings. This is the building. If I squint my eyes just right, I can see Holly Golightly sweeping up the stairway, past the step I'm sitting on now, and slipping through the door into the foyer. Paul Varjak is chasing her, a man who loves her, but Holly's intent on leaving him behind.

I can see her up in the apartment, inviting people in, one after the other, each in fabulous dresses and chic suits, filling the apartment with people, music, and fun. I see drinks flowing freely, people stealing off into the bathroom to kiss. I hear laughing and singing. I see Holly floating from guest to guest, surrounded by people she loves.

Only, when I look closer, when I see the way she closes her eyes when she talks to them, I can see something more: She doesn't love them. She's too afraid to love them. She's even too afraid to love her cat.

Because she knows that someday, everyone she loves will go away.

In my mind, I see my mother's face. So clear, like I just saw her yesterday. Like I was sitting on her lap again, and she was asking me whether I had any ideas for her to write about, and I was telling her about what was happening in my imagination. About a girl who learns how to fly, not with a jet pack or a hang glider, but with wings she sprouts from her shoulders, and how she flies to New York City. In search of something better, a place where no one dies, especially not mothers, and where everyone is as beautiful as they want to be, and everyone knows who they are. And the girl decides to fold up her wings for the last time, because she doesn't want to fly anymore, because there's nowhere else she wants to go but home.

"I sure have a story for you now, Mom," I say out loud. "I ran away."

And in my mind I hear her answer me.

Oh, Gem. Don't you know? No matter where you run, you just end up running into yourself.

5:15 A.M.

My phone buzzes and brings me back to reality. I'm still alone here, on a stoop on Seventy-first Street. A moment ago I thought it was Holly's stoop. But now, as the sky begins to lighten, I see the truth. It's just an apartment building, one they used to film some scenes in a movie fifty years ago. It's not Holly Golightly's building anymore. Maybe it never really was.

There are five texts from my father, texts I now remember ignoring last night. Last night, when I didn't want to talk to him. When I didn't want him to know where I was, or who I was. When I didn't want him to need me.

I decide to read them.

7:34 P.M.—What time will you be home, Gem? I'm ordering pizza.

10:44 P.M.—Gemma?

12:22 A.M.—Gem, I'm worried. I called Casey's and she said you aren't there. You said you'd call. Send a text if you don't want to talk to me. Just let me know you're OK. Please, Gemma.

2:22 A.M.—I miss your mother so much. I know you do, too. Come home.

I don't text back. I don't know what I would say to him right now. I don't know what I would say to anyone right now.

I miss your mother so much. I know you do, too.

I can hear his voice when I read it.

stand up, smooth out my torn skirt, and fish around in my clutch for a piece of gum. Instead, I find the itinerary.

Itinerary for the First (Annual?)
Beyond-Fabulous Breakfast at Tiffany's *Weekend!*
Saturday and Sunday, June 11–12

SATURDAY
....

❈ 6:00 A.M. ❈ *Meet at Tiffany's with pastries and coffee.*

❈ 7:00 A.M. ❈ *Breakfast at a Third Avenue diner.*

❈ 9:00 A.M. ❈ *Return to individual hotels to change.*

⚜ 10:00 A.M. ⚜ Begin walking tour of Breakfast at Tiffany's landmarks, starting at Holly's apartment building on Seventy-first Street . . .

I stare at it for a moment. It seems a lifetime ago that I handed copies of it to Bryan and Trina.

I read the last item aloud.

SUNDAY

⚜ 6:00 A.M. ⚜ Reconvene at Tiffany's for another breakfast. Decide whether to stay in New York forever, and if not, why not?

Why not?

I stare at it and read it again. More evidence that I've ruined this weekend. Not just for myself, but for Bryan and Trina and even Telly, who I didn't ever expect to care about, but now, here, in the cold morning on the hard sidewalk, I know that I do. I've even ruined it for Audrey. Which sounds stupid, I know, because she's been dead for twenty years. But she's my hero. The focus of my life ever since I first saw her picture in that magazine. And I've torn her dress.

I know what to do.

I'm going to Tiffany's.

5:30 A.M.

*J*ust like yesterday morning, there's a tiny hint of pinkish light oozing between the New York City buildings. It's soft and quiet and beautiful as it drips down from the tower tops.

I start walking toward Tiffany's. It's not that far away, but my feet are killing me.

I catch a glimpse of myself in the glass door of a bank as I walk past. No trace of Holly Golightly or Audrey Hepburn. Just *me*. I'm disheveled. My hair is all over the place, my eyeliner is smudged, and, of course, there's the torn dress, which is falling apart a little bit more with each step, the fringe feathers falling away on currents of air behind me as I walk, heavily, along the sidewalk.

Up ahead, I see a set of police barricades blocking off a side street. Behind it, men and women are putting up little white tents with tables beneath them. A street fair. One man, tall and slender, is spreading sweatpants and T-shirts on his table. I stop and watch him for a moment.

"Hello," he says.

"How much?" I ask. "For the sweats."

"Ten dollars," he says.

"And the T-shirts?"

"Five dollars. But we don't open until eight."

"Oh," I say, and I turn around to walk away.

"You want them now?" he says. He looks around. "I'm not supposed to, but . . ."

I reach into my clutch and unfold a twenty from the tightly wrapped bunch of bills. "Here," I say. "Black, please."

He puts a pair of black sweats and a black V-neck T-shirt into a plastic bag that says "I Heart New York"—it actually spells out the word *heart*.

"Shh," he says, and he takes my twenty. I stand there waiting for change, but he turns away and goes back to work. I'm obviously not getting any change.

I walk around the corner and find a doorway. I hike up the

dress and slip the sweatpants on over my shoes. I look around to see if anyone's looking before I unzip the dress and, in one quick motion, slip the dress off and the T-shirt on. I stash the dress in the "I Heart" bag and walk on, strappy black shoes clicking along the sidewalk under my baggy black sweats.

'm walking, faster now, still a few blocks from Tiffany's. My phone buzzes again. It's another text from Dusty.

I'm serious. I need that dress back.

What a jerk. He probably faked the whole thing—faked being able to afford it in the first place. Just to see if he could get me to go out with him, to jump into bed with him. And it almost worked, because I was just as big a jerk as he was. I blew off my friends for Dusty, and for a dress.

There's a sign hanging above me, swinging from a metal rod up over the sidewalk. It's faded, in old-fashioned letters, red and blue stripes down either side, like the French flag.

VIE DE FRANCE DRY CLEANING AND TAILOR. FRENCH METHOD. SAME-DAY SERVICE AND HAUTE COUTURE ALTERATIONS. SINCE 1953. HOURS: 9–6 EVERY DAY.

I turn and look at the door. In the window just to the side of the door handle is a newspaper clipping, yellowing newsprint in a black frame. I look more closely: The headline reads

FAMED FRENCH DESIGNER PRESENTS
TRUNK SHOW TO HIGH SOCIETY

It's dated 1963, and there's a photograph of a tall, sophisticated-looking man in a dark suit and close-cropped hair, holding up two hangers with a simple black dress hanging off each one. The story reads:

Couturier Hubert de Givenchy, who rarely leaves Paris, arrived in New York City Saturday to present his newest collection for the American market in an exclusive showing to a select group of customers. A who's who of New York society arrived at the show, held in the apartment of

Mrs. George W. Clark, where Monsieur de Givenchy draped models in the gowns.

"Every woman should have a little black dress," Monsieur de Givenchy said through an interpreter.

Mrs. Sanford Greenburger, a longtime client of Monsieur de Givenchy, was delighted to purchase three gowns. "I'll still travel to Paris for the collections, of course," she said.

This reporter was curious how the dresses looked so fresh after the long trip from France. Monsieur de Givenchy explained: "I send all of the dresses out for cleaning and pressing shortly after my arrival at Idlewild."

And whom does the designer trust with the task?

"Vie de France, bien sûr," de Givenchy said.

Vie de France. Exactly where I'm standing right now. What are the odds? I look up at the pink sky and think, *Thank you*. I mean it for Audrey.

I look at the "I Heart New York" bag hanging from my fingers, filled with a treasure of a dress. Made by the hands of the man in the photograph in the frame in front of me.

I hang it from the doorknob of the Vie de France dry cleaner's and text the address of the place back to Dusty. Then I delete his number from my phone.

&verything about the street outside Tiffany's this morning feels familiar. It's just like it was yesterday. The empty sidewalk. The cool air. The crawling cabs. The distant sound of a siren snaking between the buildings, singing about a distant tragedy in another part of town. The mist in the air, a cool mist that's almost prickly. The white deli bag and paper cup of coffee I have in my hand, the pastry bought at the same store I visited yesterday. The wondering if anyone else will show up.

But even if everything feels familiar, nothing is the same.

For one thing, there's my outfit, which could be comical if I'd planned it that way. Black V-neck. Black sweatpants. Black strappy heels. What would Audrey say?

That's the other thing that's different: I don't care. I look like a wreck, but it takes more than a dress to become Audrey Hepburn. I'm not Audrey. And I'm not Holly. I look at that reflection in the Tiffany's window and, this time, I see what's really there: Gemma Beasley.

My phone buzzes. It's Dad.

I don't pick up.

I walk to the edge of the curb and stand at the corner of the sidewalk, at exactly the spot where Gladiator nearly peed on my foot yesterday.

"Hold on, Dad," I say out loud. "Not yet. Soon."

I notice another cab, then another. A horn. The city is coming to life around me. I walk back toward Tiffany's and lean against the building, heavy and alone.

My shoes are killing me, the black straps digging into my cold, swollen feet. I shift from one foot to the other and back again, but it doesn't help. I raise the coffee to my lips and I wait.

6:00 A.M.

 dog barks around the corner, and another dog answers with a yap.

I scan the sidewalk. They're not here.

Of course they aren't here. There's no way they're coming. Why would they? They're pissed at me, and I don't blame them.

I'm pissed at me, too.

After the movie, the best movie of all time, they all probably went back to the Four Seasons to sleep in those deep, soft, comfortable beds, and that's where they are now, piled among the pillows, so many pillows, slowly breathing and dreaming of the room service breakfast they'll order later, to eat on the balcony overlooking the endless expanse of Central Park, and talk about how much they love New York City and how they never want to leave—why would anyone ever want to? After all, they had good reasons to want to get away from home, too. Bryan, bullied so badly. And Trina, working so hard at the Corral.

Twenty-four hours ago I would have thought: Here I am at Tiffany's, after a glamorous night out with a rich young man, just like Holly Golightly. I accepted dinner and gifts, and I met fabulous people.

If a simple pastry and a paper cup of hot coffee at the Tiffany's window is good enough for Holly Golightly, it's good enough for me.

But now I realize I was so, so wrong.

I know better now. I know what breakfast at Tiffany's really is.

It's sitting on a cold sidewalk, alone, wondering who you are, wondering why you're here, what you've done wrong, and where you're going next. And there's all that beauty so close, just beyond that window, that it seems like you can almost touch it, but really, you can't go inside. This is what Audrey Hepburn felt when she played the part in the movie. I see it now.

Having breakfast at Tiffany's isn't glamorous at all. Holly Golightly was just lost. She might not have gone to bed with all her suitors, but she paid a price for getting fifty dollars for the powder room.

6:15 A.M.

"**I**s it her?"

The voice sounds so close. So familiar. But still, I'm not sure I recognize it.

I slowly turn around from the Tiffany's window and I see them.

"It *is* her," says Telly.

"She has a lot of nerve coming back here after what she did," Trina says.

I burst into tears and slide down the side of the building till I sit. For the first time in these twenty-four hours, I cry for the mistakes I made. I cry for letting down my real friends. I cry the tears I haven't let myself cry in the months since my mother died.

"Now she cries?" Trina says. "Give me a break."

"Save it, Trina," Telly says. "Not now."

Telly leans down and touches my forearm. "Gemma," Telly asks, "are you OK?"

My eyes flicker across Telly's face, so pure and pale and white. I look up to see Bryan, magnificent Bryan, so perfectly groomed and wearing a perfectly tailored suit, tortoiseshell sunglasses, and those beautiful cognac oxfords.

"Oh, Gemma," Telly says. "Help me get her up," she says to Bryan.

Bryan leans down and drapes my arm around his neck. They stand up, and so do I, wobbling as I rise.

"I—I—I'm so glad to see you," I say.

Trina stomps a few steps away. "Tell me when you're ready to leave," she says. She turns toward the street, which is filling up with traffic.

"Look at you," Bryan says, swatting dust off my sweatpants. "Oh, Gemma. You're in sweats. Where's your dress?"

"Where do you think it is?" Trina says, walking back toward the wall but not looking at me. "She obviously left it at *his* house."

I don't answer. I don't really know exactly what to say. I

could tell them the truth, but I'm not sure they'll believe me, or care.

"Did he hurt you?" Bryan says. "Gemma?"

I shake my head no. "I'm so sorry," I say. "He didn't hurt me. I'm the only one who hurt anyone. I never should have left you."

"Whatever," Trina says.

"Trina," Bryan says. "Look at her. She's a mess."

"What?" Trina says. "Of course she's a mess. She deserves it after her little *rendezvous* last night. After ditching her friends. After lying to us! Don't look at me to help her now. If she wants help, she can just call her mother."

Her words sting in a way that I know she'll never be able to understand. "My mother," I say. "I don't have—"

But before I can finish, I stop, catching my breath in my throat, stifling a sob.

"What?" Trina asks. "What don't you have?"

Not now, I think. *Later.* "Nothing," I say. "Listen. I know I did the wrong thing last night. I know I hurt you. But I just wanted one more chance to see you. I know this is the end of our weekend. And the end of *Oh Yeah, Audrey!* Even if last night had been different, if I'd said no to Dusty, if I'd stayed with you and stuck to our plan and gone to the movie and done everything I was supposed to do—I knew this morning would still be our last chance to see one another. And I didn't want to miss it."

Trina turns around, swiftly, sharply. "You ditched us," she says. "Who does that?"

Who does that? I repeat in my head. *Holly Golightly?*

"I'm sorry," I say. "I don't expect you to forgive me. I was . . ."

"She was swept away," Bryan says, finishing my thought. He turns to me and says quietly, "But she got in over her head."

I close my eyes.

"Are you sure you're OK?" he asks.

"I am now."

"Oh, Gemma," Telly says. "It's OK." She puts her arm around my waist.

"Trina," I say.

She ignores me, so I say it louder.

"Trina, I know I got carried away. I'm sorry. I didn't mean—" I inhale sharply. "I learned what it really means to take fifty dollars for the powder room," I say.

She doesn't answer.

"I know what it's like."

"Tell us, Gemma," Trina says, challenging me. "Tell us what it means to take fifty dollars for the powder room. Tell us what it's really like to be the *fabulous* Holly Golightly in her *fabulous* dress. *Please*. Enlighten us."

I look down at my feet, then up at the Tiffany's sign. I don't have exactly the words to say.

"That's what I thought," Trina says. "Come on, you guys."

"Wait," Telly says.

"It's lonely," I say. "It's cold. It's exhausting. It's . . ."

"What?" Trina asks.

"It's *empty*," I say, and I feel a tear drop onto my cheek. "I don't want to be Holly anymore. Or even Audrey," I say. "Just Gemma."

No one says anything for a moment. The three of them stand around me, looking at me, at my pathetic self in my pathetic sweatpants with my tousled hair and smudged makeup.

"Just Gemma."

Trina sighs. "Gemma was always enough for us," she says.

Hearing her say that makes me smile. It's a weak smile, but it's a smile. "I have something to tell you," I say.

"What is it?" Bryan says.

"My mother was a writer," I begin quietly. "She wrote stories. She loved stories. She especially loved *my* stories. The crazy stories I made up in my head. She was always so happy to hear them."

"*Was?*" Telly says.

"Was," I say.

My three friends are silent.

"I wish she was here to listen to this story," I say. "I wish I could tell it to her. I don't know if she'd even believe it—believe that I pretty much ran away from home to have breakfast at Tiffany's."

"Wait, what do you mean, you 'wish she was here' . . . ," Trina starts.

"Oh, Gemma." Bryan pulls me into a hug. "Why didn't you tell us? You never said . . ."

"I'm sorry," I say.

Telly grabs my shoulders and tears slip down my cheeks again. "I was afraid you'd treat me differently. And I didn't want you to see me as some sad and needy girl, sitting at home alone with her depressed dad, writing on her blog, feeling sorry for herself. It was easier to just talk about Audrey."

"When did it happen?" Telly asks.

"A few months ago, pretty much right when I started the blog. I guess I needed something to help me escape from my real life."

"We all did," Bryan says.

"Yes," Trina says. "We all did."

"I know," I say. I sniffle.

Telly pulls a Kleenex from her backpack and hands it to me.

"But we're here for you now, Gemma, just like we always were," Bryan says. "We're all here for one another. Aren't we? Audrey just brought us together."

"I promise never to ditch you for another one of Audrey's ten-thousand-dollar dresses ever again. If you'll forgive me?"

"Deal," Telly says.

"Come on, guys," Trina says and grabs my hand. "I'm starving. Let's go to the diner."

e're sitting in the same diner we sat in yesterday, poking at plates of pancakes and stirring packets of sugar into our coffees.

"You should have been there," Bryan says. "The crowd went crazy when the opening credits came up. Everyone was humming 'Moon River' while Holly was shuffling across the sidewalk to look at the Tiffany's windows."

"And the girls behind us, they recited every single line along with the movie," Telly says. "At first it was annoying, but then—"

"They got a few lines wrong," Bryan says. "Like when Holly was having those bad dreams and yelling for Fred?"

"Yeah," Trina says. "You would have gotten them right, Gemma." She smiles at me, almost, sort of a half smile that doesn't say much. But it's the first smile she's given me this morning.

Maybe she'll forgive me. I know she's mad, but maybe, maybe we'll be the friends we were always supposed to be. I know I've changed since yesterday. I know more about . . . everything. I smile back at Trina.

"Thanks," I say, and for a moment, I feel like Holly Golightly, having her happy ending with Paul Varjak and Cat in *Breakfast at Tiffany's*. But this is *my* happy ending. And it's real.

I feel my phone vibrate in my clutch. I know it's Dad. I reach into my purse, then hold the phone in my hand for a long moment.

One buzz. Two. Three.

"I have to take this, you guys," I say.

Bryan smiles.

I get up from the booth, walk out the front door of the diner, and finally answer the phone.

....

ACKNOWLEDGMENTS

....

Thanks to Tamar Brazis, Dan Mandel, Brenda Bowen, Maria Middleton, Susan Van Metre, Jason Wells, Jim Armstrong, Andy Fishering, Paul Zakris, Pizzeria Locale, Hubert de Givenchy, Truman Capote, and Audrey Hepburn.

Tucker Shaw is the author of many popular books for teens, including *The Girls*, *Confessions of a Backup Dancer*, *Flavor of the Week*, and *Anxious Hearts*. He lives in Boston, where he is an editor at *America's Test Kitchen*.